Goose River Anthology, 2015

Edited by

Deborah J. Benner

Goose River Press
Waldoboro, Maine

Library of Congress Card Number: 2015947151

ISBN: 978-1-59713-162-9

First Printing, 2015

Cover photo by Diane C. Reitz

Published by
Goose River Press
3400 Friendship Road
Waldoboro ME 04572
e-mail: gooseriverpress@roadrunner.com
www.gooseriverpress.com

Authors Included

Authors Included

Authors Included

Dedicated to

Mothers

Goose River Anthology, 2015

Mary Jo Balistreri
Genesee Depot, WI

Memorial Day

My father places them before me on the maple table in the kitchen, artifacts from his navy years—his personal experience of WWII. Packed and hidden behind stacked boxes in the attic, they are his seventy-year-old secret. At ninety, he has decided either that I am ready to hear about them, or that he is ready to tell. Perhaps both.

I finger silver dog tags as smooth as stones scoured and polished by river currents, note the faded words of his letters to my mother, the blank windows where a censor's scissors tried to obscure any observation that might give the squad's position away. Two pocket-sized books, black and somewhat ominous, lay flat and dense begging to be opened, for their contents to finally spill out.

Anxiety becomes a presence as Dad leaves the room, giving me the space to explore, and my thoughts to roam. As children, when we asked about it, Dad deflected the questions.

We had learned not to ask.

I open to the slanted script and begin to read. The ink is smeared in places, and I imagine his hand trembling, or perhaps tears falling. He writes of decimated Japanese villages, little kids lost and crying, bodies in the rice paddies, bodies huddled together in fear—the killing of them out of fear.

I don't realize how tightly I'm gripping the book until the beads of my own sweat drip onto the page. Loosening my hold, I wonder about the possible tears. I never saw Dad cry. Yet as I continue reading into the second book, I hear the uncertain, quivering voice that haunts these pages. It is as jarring as the assured and positive voice coming from the living room as Kate Smith sings "God Bless America."

Pausing to catch my breath, I look up and out of the window, notice the stripes of red, white, and blue that were

Mary Jo Balistreri
Genesee Depot, WI

uplifted this morning now hanging limp in the afternoon desert, the street emptied by heat. The wave of happiness that seemed to float up out of nowhere is replaced by something heavy and hobbled with time. The Sousa marches that stirred the early morning air from band practice at the rec center are replaced by images, death-stilled and sun-hollowed. How does one reconcile the spirited and robust music of patriotism with killing for one's flag?

Putting the books down to get an iced tea, I recall the Memorial Days we celebrated when I was a child: Dad home from work, and Mother planting sweet William and bachelor buttons, us kids full of energy and excitement for the picnic we'd have later—all the strawberry ice cream we could eat. And though we knew the day was set-aside for veterans and those who died in previous wars, there was no mention of it in our home, no discussion of anything that could throw a pall on the day. Memorial Day was a concept, but it meant something else in reality. It was the unofficial beginning of summer, a holiday of celebration, but not reflection.

Even as an adult, Memorial Day was Ocean City, New Jersey on the boardwalk: Philly cheese steaks, caramel corn, crashing waves, seaweed, cinnamon buns, and salt-water taffy.

I put these memories aside as I continue to read the names Dad wrote down of the men who died, the handwriting becoming more illegible, followed by whole pages of nothing, then again the names of wounded men in his squad—men he would never see again. I hear loneliness and loss, in spite of the entries about the band he sang with on board his ship. I see the young man in the photo, yellowed and unmoored from its scotch tape. He is bare-chested wearing a grass skirt, a knife clasped in his mouth. *This is my dad?*

In the living room, Dad waits for my return as he sits in his chair with a glass of Merlot. I walk in and he offers me a glass of wine, which I eagerly accept.

"Well," he says. "What do you think?"

Mary Jo Balistreri
Genesee Depot, WI

I pause and then say, "You went through so much. Why did you carry this burden all alone? Seventy years, Dad? Didn't it bother you, eat away at your personal peace?"

He shrugs and replies, "There was no way to talk about it. The war was over; I wanted to start fresh. You were too young and how would talking about it have changed anything, except spoil the new memories we were making?"

We sit for a while on the road from one life to another. The peach shears change the sun's glare to amber as we contemplate the echo of so many lives. A poet recites Whitman's "Vigil Strange I Kept on the Field One Night" as background music fills in the spaces with something I don't know— maybe Charles Ives' "Declaration Day."

In the shifting sheet of light, my initial feeling is sadness. How torn Dad must have been by these experiences, but also how saddened I am by the knowledge that such a large chunk of his life had been unavailable, the next thought tumbling over that one—I wonder if knowing would have made a difference? What would it have meant in terms of life-shaping events and how it affected Dad? As a child, wouldn't I have been more inclined to just listen to the facts like I would a sad bedtime story? I vaguely wonder too if he still believes in war but I dismiss that thought. I know what he would say: *We were attacked. There was no choice.*

With dawning awareness, I realize it is that same instinct that silenced his voice all these years because there was no choice. Speaking the truth could not have made anyone's life better. When Dad was a young man, tears were not allowed; he did what he could. My eyes brim with the tears he had hidden between the pages of a diary, with what he endured for his family, to protect us as he had protected our country. And I think, for the first time consciously, *My dad is a hero—* even in his silence.

My dad is a hero.

I walk over to his chair and put my arms around him. *Thank you* is all I can manage to say as the Mormon

Mary Jo Balistreri
Genesee Depot, WI

Tabernacle Choir raises their voices as one, builds to a full
crescendo, and fills the house from one corner to the other
with "America the Beautiful."

***

Anne W. Hammond
Woolwich, ME

The Woodcutter's Wish

Do not go gentle into the forest dark;
Chain saw and skidder split open the day.
Slash, slash against the tattered forest arc.

Skidders rumble down roads in the forest park;
Drag a ditch, make puddles on the way.
Do not go gentle into the forest dark.

Quartered trees bound for fire place dark,
Fallen hemlocks steal deer feeding spots away
Slash, slash against the tattered arc.

Yard logs sorted in piles by the mark
Firewood, saw logs, pulp to travel one way.
Do not go gentle into the forest dark.

Branches are sundered, lie broken as bark,
Heaped for deer, for nesting birds to stay.
Slash, slash against the tattered forest arc.

Woodcutters drop trees as if on a lark.
Finished loggers buck the harvest away.
Do not go gentle in the forest dark
Slash, slash against the tattered forest arc.

Tom Crowley
Lincolnville, ME

Snow Melt

The snow melts, revealing secrets
An empty bottle, thrown
April is the cruelest month
The old man died alone.

He waited through the winter
His wife had left him there.
But he could not bear the spring
Watching her garden, bare.

The ground was thawing daily
It would soon be time to plant
He stared out of the window
His memory fading, scant.

The harvest would be slim this year
He dug the hole quite deep
He climbed inside, close to her
And laid his head down, to sleep.

The snow melt dripped down jagged sides
His face got wet and grave.
He climbed back out and got a tarp
From his boat *Be Not Afraid*

She would not sail, he could not row.
They agreed to separate paths.
Him to sail and her to grow.
That year would be their last.

Tom Crowley
Lincolnville, ME

Each day he left, sail bag in hand.
He waved as he crossed the field
To step his mast and ply the waves
Neither wished to yield.

The corn grew well, the wind died down
She weeded, sowed, and reaped
He put his canvas sails away
And met her in the keep.

They knelt beside the brussel sprouts
He pulled the wrong thing twice.
She kissed him on the top of his head
And said, "Water would be nice."

He rose, brushed off his soiled knees
It was harder now, to stand.
Returning to her side, he sat,
A glass of water in his hand.

She laughed, that wondrous smile beamed
He laughed too at the joke.
They sat together on the ground
The air cool, smelling of wood smoke.

The snows then came, the jars were opened,
Butter beans, peas and corn.
The boat was covered with the tarp
The wood stacked in the barn.

She slept, like death, arose no more
They found them both in bed.
A gentle smile on her face
He slept on, like the dead.

Tom Crowley
Lincolnville, ME

There was no funeral, children gone.
Her ashes were in a Ball jar.
He sprinkled them on her flower bed
By the back door, not too far.

But here he was, close to her
Like she always wanted him to be.
He wondered if she felt him there
As the wind rose on the sea.

He stood up in the grave
To take one last look around.
And saw a gull perched on the boat
And a crow walking on the ground.

"Be gone!" he cried, to scare them off
"I am trying to rest in my grave!"
The last words he saw were on the stern:
And read "Be Not Afraid."

***

Gerry Di Gesu
West Chatham, MA

Fear of Flying

Over capricious sheets of foam
flight I ache to share
feet planted on a sturdy board
the windsurfer's lone translucent wing
grabs the wind—
soars   flies   leap-frogs
across roiling steel-gray seas
racing clouds to the horizon

Jean Biegun
Manitowoc, WI

Summer Sky Kids

Pied piper of leeches,
barefoot kid in a June creek,
scientist eager
to test them on skin.

Blue teeth berry picker,
ponytailed rainbow spotter,
milkweed surveyor
counting monarch eggs.

Copycat caller
of campground frog songs,
tent flap stargazer,
guardian to fireflies.

Sharp-grass dunes hopper,
sand fortress builder,
stone skipper, dirt pile digger,
forest trail guide.

Decoder of cloud shapes,
collector of hail stones,
artist of adventure
in summer sun.

Diana Coleman
Rockland, ME

Glimpses of Kenya from a Mzungu Woman

Bumping along in an old Toyota van over dusty "roads" with huge holes, we arrived in the bush where the Samburu live, many hours north of Nairobi.   There I met two girls—"D" and "S"—from poor families with drunken fathers. Guessing they were nine or ten years old, neither girl had been outside her village or had attended school. They did not want to marry—their destiny at the time. They wanted to go to school. Taken in temporarily by our host family, the girls spoke Samburu, not the native language Kiswahili. Surrounded by mud huts and thorn bushes, we, the mzungus (white persons), camped in tents in the sand on our host's property.

Early one morning, as roosters crowed under a radiant pink sky, D stood staring into the van's side mirror. Entranced, she looked at her reflection. I was drawn to D, a spunky girl with a big smile. We taught her how to write her name in English. She was excited to hold a pencil and form letters on paper. The girls needed sponsors or would be forced back to their homes and be wed. I committed to helping support D with school and boarding fees. Another woman agreed to find a sponsor for S who had run away. Though a drunkard who wanted his daughter married, D's father came to where we were, gave his permission to take her to a boarding school, and shook my hand; her mother came separately, thanked me, and gave me her beaded necklace.

We attended community meetings under an enormous acacia tree. The men and women from the bush gathered separately to discuss female genital cutting (FGC) led by two Kenyans—a Turkana man and a Samburu woman. They explained that FGC was now illegal in Kenya in 2011. The men, draped in red checked shukas (blankets) and colorful fabrics, understood that girls undergoing "the cut" may jeop-

Diana Coleman
Rockland, ME

ardize their health or life, depriving men of having boys.
They agreed that sex was better with uncircumcised, versus
circumcised, women and girls. The revered elder announced
that the men must ensure this practice is discontinued.
Another day, the women, wrapped in colorful kangas (fabric
used as a skirt, shawl or dress) and wearing intricate plate-
like beaded necklaces, bracelets and earrings, ululated (a
powerful high pitched tongue trill), sang and danced. They
prayed for rain. The Samburu woman accompanying us
talked to them about FGC. The women vowed to continue
this long-time cultural tradition, an important girl's initiation
rite. Girls who were talked to in school favored eliminating
the practice. While outlawed, FGC continues in rural areas
like this village. It will take time before the women no longer
perform the girls' circumcisions.

Driving by van to the boarding school was an eye-pop-
ping experience for D and S who had never ridden in a vehi-
cle or been away from their village. We stayed overnight in a
modest, stucco hotel in Isiolo. Sitting on plastic chairs in the
inner courtyard, which opened to the sky, the girls stared—
mesmerized by the box mounted in the corner near the ceiling. "How come the people are so small? How did they get
into the box?" they asked. The Samburu woman translated.
The girls had never seen a TV. As the sky grew dark, S
became frightened seeing lights on. "What happened to the
sun?" she wanted to know, staring at a light bulb. We went
into the room where they would sleep. I took them into the
bathroom and demonstrated how to use and flush a toilet.
They jumped back startled by the sound and swirling water.
They had never seen a bed. "Why will we sleep off the
ground? Will we fall off?" They shook their heads and stared
at me. The girls slept together and clung to each other all
night. Eating in a restaurant, they picked up the utensils.
"What are they?" They devoured ugali, their food staple—a
sticky paste made from cooked maize (corn) flour and
water—and eaten with hands. D tried a French fry and spit

Diana Coleman
Rockland, ME

it out. Told it was potato, she ate all of them.

We took a circuitous route to see giraffes, zebras, elephants, dik-diks (small antelopes), guinea fowl, ibis, weavers (yellow birds with round nests that hang like lanterns from acacia trees) and more. D had extraordinary vision and saw animals long before we did. She repeatedly hit my arm, pointed excitedly and laughed. Camping the next night at a deserted safari resort, the girls watched us pitch tents. We ate delicious grilled goat, killed by local Maasai warriors. They hung it from a tree and gracefully finessed the butchering. Like Giacometti sculptures, the tall thin men wore shirts and red plaid fabric from their waists to ankles—the young warriors donned a string of colorful beads crossed over their chests and no shirts. Happy to sleep on the ground in a colorful nylon house to themselves, the girls whispered and giggled into the night. Lions roared and coyotes howled in the distance.

After enrolling the girls in the children's boarding school, we headed to the cramped uniform shop with a list of mandatory supplies and clothing. Isiolo is a run down, bustling town with faded painted stucco buildings surrounded by sand. Young boys staggered around—delirious from sniffing pungent glue out of filthy whiskey bottles. The girls had only what they wore—D, a faded Coco Lounge shirt and skirt; S, a torn and soiled school uniform a teacher had salvaged. Smiling, they modeled new crisp white blouses, bright blue dresses and royal blue v-neck sweaters. The salesman laid pastel underpants, decorated with flowers and butterflies, on the scratched glass counter. The girls looked at me. I pantomimed putting the panties on over my feet and up my legs.

D and S tittered in response. With mattresses, socks, underpants, uniforms, soap and shoes (a change from bare feet and flip-flops), they were ready to begin school.

After my second trip to Kenya in 2012, D and S were moved to different children's homes in western Kenya. There was a hostile take-over by new staff in their first home and

Diana Coleman
Rockland, ME

the girls reported mistreatment. The region was engulfed in sporadic outbreaks of violence with invading Somalis burning villages and killing people. There was strife between Kenyan tribes as well. On my third visit to Kenya for the month of March 2014, I traveled around on my own. I only saw a few mzungus in the capital the entire time. There was a dearth of tourists since the Westgate Mall terrorist attack in Nairobi in fall 2013. Not planning on being on the east coast where new outbreaks of violence occurred, I wasn't too concerned.

Traveling by bus, we passed rusted corrugated steel shacks selling gum, sweets and cell phone time cards; women sitting in the dirt behind artistically balanced displays of potatoes and tomatoes; school children in uniform; women walking erectly, arms by their sides, huge urns and bundles balanced on their heads; old and young men; and goats, donkeys, cows and chickens meandering along the road. Bright red, blue, yellow, green and orange painted stucco shops advertised Coca-Cola, Safari Com (cell phone communications), Kaluma (a pain-relieving cream) and Doublemint Gum.

Taking a local matatu (public van) overflowing with babies, banana bunches, bags of potatoes and kale inside and hanging off the roof, I arrived at the children's home founded by Bev Stone, a Maine mzungu woman with Expanding Opportunities. It was in rural Mangu near the city of Nakuru. Initially shy when she saw me, D became talkative when showing me her schoolbooks. She has grown tall—a beautiful young woman who now speaks fluent Kiswahili, good English and studies math, religion, English, science and history. Older when she started primary school, D is in a level with younger children. Self-assured, she is doing well in her subjects.

The compound has separate boys and girls dorms, a large dining room used as a study hall and meeting room, and a kitchen. Unusual for this rural area, there is electric-

Diana Coleman
Rockland, ME

ity in the buildings. Rainwater is collected in large cisterns. There is a shamba (garden) and goats and chickens roam about. The children's diet is primarily ugali, beans, greens and pasta. They drink hot spaghetti water with their pasta, which was topped with small brown beans and onions. The cook was shocked to learn that at home, I toss out pasta water. He uses every drop—as a hot drink, soup stock or sauce base.

D and I attended a long church service together on Sunday. The minister asked me to speak. Saying a few Kiswahili words and phrases until my repertoire ran out, I added in English that I came from "Obama Land" (to laughter and cheers), was pleased to be there and thanked them for their hospitality.

Leaving Mangu, I headed by matatu to southwestern rural Kenya to the village of Igare. *The Daily Nation's* front-page photo that morning showed passengers killed on a flipped matatu on the same steep, curvy road we would be taking. Undeterred by this accident, our driver took sharp turns at high speed. The lush green countryside rushed past—sugar cane, avocado, banana, papaya and mango trees, and hillsides covered with shiny-leafed tea bushes.

There, I spent a couple of weeks at another children's home and two schools run by Marcella Ogega, a gregarious, cheerful woman from Kenya's Gusii tribe. I joined over 100 vibrant, resilient women who meet weekly as part of the Mpanzi ("to nurture from seed") organization that Marcella and her three daughters founded. All of the women have been abused and many are married to drunken, polygamist husbands. Raised in severe poverty, Marcella struggled while married to a drunken, abusive man who died young. Formerly humiliated by her husband and mother-in-law for having no sons, she now thrives and is successful. Her three daughters have college and advanced degrees.

The women persevere and support each other with violence prevention programs and enterprising ventures—rais-

Diana Coleman
Rockland, ME

ing goats and chickens; renting plastic chairs for events; and purchasing solar lights to replace smelly, smoky kerosene lamps in their homes. Rearing children; they plant and nurture shambas; and walk long distances to market to sell tomatoes, potatoes, greens and onions. They scrape together money to buy tea, cow's milk for chai, sugar and maize and pay fees to send their daughters to school. Educating girls is the best way to improve their lives—to avoid early marriage and bearing children at a young age.

I taught "Life Skills" and "Creative Arts" classes (made bracelets and necklaces from glow in the dark rubber bands I brought) and led the children in song with verses about their lives to "Row, Row, Row Your Boat" with gestures they made up. It was the first time they ever sang in rounds, which they thought was hilarious. The children sang over and over, their exuberant voices echoing off the courtyard walls:

> *We read, write and do our maths,*
> *And then we take our tests!*
> *Merrily, merrily, merrily, merrily,*
> *We want to be the best!*
>
> *We eat, eat, eat our food,*
> *To make us nice and strong!*
> *Ugali, Ugali, Ugali, Ugali,*
> *And that's the end of our song!*

Blending in with my ghostly face among dark faces was impossible. Yelling "mzungu," children pointed when they saw me walking around the village. Carefully approaching me with one index finger held out, they touched my extended hand. They quickly shrunk back, laughed and ran away. Curious to know what white skin feels like, others followed. Sometimes they shook my hand. Older people stared until I said, "Jambo! Habieri?" (Hello; How are you?). Then, seri-

Diana Coleman
Rockland, ME

ous faces lit up with broad smiles showing beautiful, shining white teeth and responded. I replied, "Masuri sana" (Very fine) and "Asante sana" (Thank you very much). Kiswahili is a melodic language with words and phrases like "Sawa-sawa" (Okay) and "La la salama" (Have a peaceful sleep).

Fortunate to visit Kenya three times, I only glimpsed at their culture and appreciated the warmth and hospitality of the people I met. Playing, singing, dancing and laughing, we shared stories, talked about common issues and corrected misperceptions—e.g. all Americans are *no*t rich; domestic violence *does* exist in the United States; and Africa is *not* a country.

Marcella visited Maine in June 2013, with her daughter Jackie and grandchildren. Hosted by my Rockland neighbors Ann (who visited Kenya with me in 2012), and her husband Gary, they served lobster—a local delicacy. Marcella watched as the large, bluish-black creatures, with bulging black eyes, squirming multiple legs and banded claws, were thrown into boiling water. Emerging from the pot a brilliant red, a lobster was plunked down on her plate. Shocked, she stared at it and shook her head. Together, we laughed and agreed we defined "Chakula kizuri"—"Delicious meal"—differently.

***

Sylvia Little-Sweat
Wingate, NC

Lotus

In spring's quickening
frogs fall silent in the night
under lotus moons.

Michelle M. Faith
Camden, ME

A Place for Everything

At Aslanden on Belleau Lake,
the water laps against the dock,
hummingbirds hover at the fuchsia,
and at night the northern lights
play across the black floor of the sky
like gossamer scarves
shimmering from a dancer's hand.

Up at the house, name cards read
like a family litany
above two rows of towels—
indigo, burgundy, forest green—
hanging on wooden pegs.
On any given day,
you know who's about
by the dampness of their towels.

For years not a dry one
was to be found all summer long.
Now, even mid-season, some
stay bone-dry for weeks.
Children grow up, lead lives
of their own, make other commitments.

Yet the towels endure,
thick and sturdy and resilient,
useful to those present,
holding a place for those absent—
like the place held at seder
for the prophet Elijah
in hopes he will come again.

Jon Potter
Rockport, ME

Winter: Rockport Harbor

The fresh brookwater floats over the harbor's salt
And slowly freezes, thin at first,
Then thickens, greys, ice-flat—
Sealing down the dance of waves
And gripping firm the few boats left.
Beneath the flat, the weeds, the fish
Are slowed, stilled.

The tide slides the flat slowly up and down the shore
Smearing the rocks dull with ice.

We're like this harbor.
Our spring is lively; birds flutter, jump, swim.
Ideas like fish crowd, flip, slide.
Summer is exploring,
Finding joy in the new near the old.
The weeds bubble, flutter, cohere.
Fall-time slows; brash cold winds push winter in.
Then the ice floats, flattens,
Seals memories, blocks movement,
Connecting moments.

Grey and hard.
Thickening.

Ann M. Penton
Green Valley, AZ

Reunion Dream

Stiff, life-sized, flat—
paper doll on a popsicle stick

My father-figure in black and white,
suddenly set against a backdrop of green Colorado

Twisted sideways all these years since his death,
so I barely saw even the thin edge

Rotated last night—
face on, Dad again held my chubby little hand

***

State Poetry Convention

Haiku in their simple strapless formals mingle.
Trying to get into the spirit,
they join in the sometimes-boisterous,
rowdy toasts of beer offered by the ballads,
all decked out in their bulky attire.

Christine Chamberlain
Brunswick, ME

Assignation

She closed the book, placed it on the table and, finally, walked through the door. Settling into the back seat of the taxi, she reviewed her morning. Things had been much as usual. Mr. Curtis' garage doors had rumbled up, just as they did every morning at six o'clock. At 6:30 the newspaper had slapped against her porch. At seven, the school bus had arrived to pick up the children across the street.

Yes, she had lain in bed longer than usual. Eventually rising, she had moved into the bathroom. Catching a glimpse of her body in the mirror, she had reflected how slender she was now, just the way Tom had always wanted her to be. But that was in the past. He had not been patient enough.

No need to wash her hair this morning, that was one good thing. Moving to the bureau, she had chosen underwear, lingering over her brassieres. Something fancy, she had wondered to herself; something plain; no bra at all? This was new territory. She had settled for no bra. Pants, slacks, and her favorite blue blouse. Blue was for hope. No jewelry. Should she wear perfume for something like this? Less was best, she decided. No trappings.

Bed made, a quick check of the rooms, tidy and clean, just in case. It was hard to tell how days like this would end. Down the stairs, no coffee this morning, but her flowered chair catching the morning sun had looked inviting. A few minutes of reading wouldn't hurt, she had decided. She was early. Her small suitcase sat by the door. A negligee, make-up, slippers, underwear, toothbrush. That should do it. She would either be back in a few days or, perhaps, she mused, not at all.

Sitting by the window, she had wondered what he was doing this morning, that man who would see her body, touch her breasts, reassure her that all would be well. He was a

Christine Chamberlain
Brunswick, ME

stranger in many ways, someone she barely knew yet someone who knew her intimately, perhaps as no man had ever
known her.

Minutes had passed, her book of poetry lying idle on her
lap. At last, rubbing her hand over her smooth skull, she had
reached for the silk scarf by the chair. Now, nestling down in
the leather seat in the back of the taxi, she slipped her hand
inside her blouse with an absent-minded gesture, fluttering
her fingers around her bare breasts, whispering goodbye.

***

Janice Babcock
Wauwatosa, WI

Sudden Death 50 Years Ago

Daytime blizzard
After job home clean-up
No snow blowers invented
Hand shoveling needed

Too much for his heart
Only in his 60's
Dad didn't make it
No hospital for him

My degree just earned
We were three now two
Family plans abandoned

Now a huge hole

Genie Dailey
Jefferson, ME

Kinship with the Sea

Ever changing yet eternally the same—
Ocean calls us to observe, to see our lives
Reflected in her rhythm.

Tides of love, compassion, joy,
Great swells of feeling flood and fill us.
Then comes the ebbing,
Ocean out-flowing,
We're leveled and languid, quiescent on shore.

Storms of anger, surging sadness,
White-capped waves of worry can claim us.
But ocean becalms,
Settles and saves us;
We float at peace once more.

We share a kinship with the sea—
Sometimes rough waters, more often smooth sailing;
Ever changing yet eternally the same,
Ocean speaks to us of living
In rhythm with the tides.

Sherry Ballou Hanson
Portland, OR

The Blessing of the Fleet 4/30/2000

In honor of the proud
independent Maine fishermen
who lost their lives at sea.
—Fishermen's Memorial
Boothbay Harbor, Maine

Who would have thought
My sister and I would stumble
On the blessing of the fleet
On a dock behind a warehouse
In Boothbay Harbor, Maine.

Surely Our Lady Queen of Peace
Gathers her robes close
When a raw wind
Rips across the bay,
But she watches over Elizabeth,
Jubilee, the Aaron and Sarah
Rocking on the water
As they come for the blessing.

The clergy slants into the wind
Praying for the souls
Of the men, a priest
And a rabbi, a minister
Of God, praying
For fish in the nets,
Safety on the water
When men go to sea.

Anne L. Hess
Stillwater, ME

Bat Cat and Robin

Robin didn't know she was a dog. She was named after a bird, and had long sleek feather-like fur; she could leap up high and sail gracefully over fences just like the flighty little things she could've eaten in a single bite, so what else was she to think? She wasn't very good at that nest-thing, though, so at times she wondered—in that slow-thinking dog way—what she was. Some days she thought she was a human, and there was no way to talk her out of it then. She couldn't count, so the two extra limbs didn't seem significant. Neither did she appreciate that her ears were far too large for a human, and her nose infinitely more sensitive. Or that her skin was covered with rich, cashmere-soft wavy fur that humans loved to put their hands in, whereas those same humans had no fur at all.

Batcat, on the other hand, thought she was a dog. After all, her earliest memories were of snuggling up to her soft, furry friend that she thought was her mama. Mama's purr didn't sound just right, though, and sometimes she yelled awfully loudly. But her mama would let her curl up in the curve of her belly, or wrap her long, graceful black tail around Batcat in such a reassuring way that Batcat was *positive* Robin was her mother. A human might have mistaken her for a bat, with that black mask across her forehead and nose, even though she had no wings; and how could they account for the large white patches of fur on her body? It was a beautiful body, gleaming white against dark, dark black, slender but muscular like her cousin the lion. Batcat could flatten herself against the ground, creep on her belly in a stalk, and pounce without warning just as good as her giant cousins. She just didn't know those were characteristics of big cats, not big dogs; she would have been mortified to be compared to the despised hyena clan.

Anne L. Hess
Stillwater, ME

And so Batcat began her dog lessons. How to sniff along the floor, how to greet another dog properly, how to run and leap and chase, and how to groom her mama and those other creatures, you know, those two-legged servants that hung around the house; how to drool enough to evoke pity, and therefore, food. She learned how to jump up into a lap and nestle there while being groomed by the servant. She learned how to steal food from a high platform, how to find fresh potted vegetables, and how to mark her territory. She was brave, too, eager to attack any living thing in her path when her mood was sour.

Batcat learned how to bite, too, using those big ripping canines of hers to snag her prey, then disembowel them with those scythe-like rear paws. She got very good at biting, so good that she became as fierce as her large relatives that lived on the savannah. Unfortunately, sometimes she bit her mama, and her primary servant, too. That didn't go over very well, not well at all, and she definitely didn't like the ensuing scoldings.

Life for Batcat and Robin wasn't all a bowl of cherries; sometimes they had to put up with strange invaders, annoying babies; with loneliness, and boredom especially when the servants were gone. There were times of belly pain, aching paws and muscles, matted fur and rashes, and bad teeth. Of fear and insomnia. And the sticky place! They wrestled you around with a tight grip, then actually stuck you with thorns! Or shaved off your beautiful fur, or poked pills down your throat. Dastardly. Except for their very own pack/pride, humans were not to be trusted.

Robin had her own cross to bear. Instead of her rightful purpose in life as a glamour queen, courted by all the handsome males at the dog conventions, she was banished to the mundane realm of humans. How degrading, she once thought, to be a mere pet. Why can't I be the one to have all those adorable little babies to raise and show off? Am I not good enough, she asked herself? Her humans made her feel

Anne L. Hess
Stillwater, ME

good, but that wasn't a good substitute for a virile lover.

She became the noble sentry, the guardian who paced the perimeter and signaled any danger or intruder. She was diligent in her duties, especially when her humans were asleep; she knew how vulnerable they were without good teeth for attacking, good hearing to detect an imminent raid, or loud voices or good running speed. Of course, if danger really appeared, she retreated quickly to the safest place she could find: behind the legs of her human. She was a sentinel, not a soldier, and she wasn't the bravest dog in the kennel. Loving, yes, not brave.

Batcat was the opposite. She thought, with her tiny little brain, that she was big, huge, terrifying, and could vanquish the greatest foe. She succeeded, as long as the foe was no larger than a mouse. Or vole. Or baby chipmunk. She didn't know how small she was, how puny her voice was, or how much slower she was than even the slowest bird. Fortunately, because she only got out of her house twice, she never had the chance to prove her skills as a huntress. And that was a good thing, at least for the birds.

When Batcat first arrived in Robin's den, she thought she was her baby puppy who needed nursing and nurturing, and that she had finally joined a pack. The wee thing was so lost, so small and helpless, and with such a plaintive cry. So she dutifully groomed her (much to Batcat's dismay), nipped and chased her, and played tag and ball with her. She let Batcat play with her tail, and would playfully swat her with it, quite firmly knocking her head over heels. Batcat would wait behind a door, totally silent in the manner of cats, and then pounce wildly on Robin when she walked by. She would run after Robin, nipping at her furry britches with delight.

Robin would have taken care of Batcat in the dark of night—when her own vision wasn't very good—but Batcat wanted to play at night! It's time for sleeping, you little brat, Robin would think. Settle down and go to sleep! Honestly, I don't know what to do with you!

Anne L. Hess
Stillwater, ME

The Great Adventure

This started the second time Batcat got out of the house. It was mid-winter, a gray day with no love in it. There had been a big snowstorm the night before, and the world, as Batcat and Robin knew it, was covered in a thick white blanket. From her window perch, Batcat thought it looked like a field of down or newly-fluffed cotton, so soft and inviting. She imagined herself floating on it, or scampering from little hillock to hillock, prancing about like a piece of down herself. She pictured soaring gracefully as she skimmed the little bumps and loosened flights of snowflakes which she could snatch with her quick tongue. She longed to be out there.

Robin knew what fresh snow was like: it was cold! She'd been out to use her special bathroom, and walked in the slippery, treacherous stuff, feeling like her poor paws were going to freeze and fall right off her legs. The snow was deep enough that she could barely get her hind quarters down far enough not to pee on herself, or smear poop on her rear. Her britches were a source of pride for her, and she hated getting them soiled. But you had to do what had to be done, like it or not. She didn't like it. Why couldn't she have an indoor toilet like Batcat, she would have asked her humans if she'd known how.

Winter does strange things in a northern state like theirs, and some so incredible that you wouldn't believe it if you hadn't seen them for yourself. The power of winter frost is amazing: it lifts roads, rocks, and buildings several inches off their bases. It contorts and warps any angle that tries to be square, and creates giant moguls that sets your car into a mid-air lunge, only to drop you rudely into the next gully.

The frost had had its way with Robin's and Batcat's house, so all of the doors were out of kilter; the windows had been locked in place since November, and no one dared open them because they wouldn't close again until summer. There were snow piles against the house so high that a house-

Anne L. Hess
Stillwater, ME

bound animal might not be able to see over them, to see what was out there. That made them all the more enticing with dreams of sliding gleefully down slippery hills or burrowing under the snow for a tasty morsel.

It was completely understandable that the outside "airlock" door wouldn't close completely, but it was unexpected that it stayed open so wide, held by a large chunk of ice that had fallen off the roof. When Robin returned from her outside business, the human didn't notice that the door stayed ajar.

Batcat was on one of her daytime trips for a snack and bathroom break, an occasion which she regularly used to peruse the territory. She often sat on her table-top perch and watched the birds come and go from the feeder, oblivious to being observed by one of their mortal enemies. Ordinarily, Batcat would not have been a menace, as she could only helplessly gaze with longing at potential prey. She could imagine the juicy, tender flesh and crunchy bones, but had no way to get them.

Until that fateful day. After using her bathroom, she was meandering back to her flapping door to return to her snoozing when she spotted the partly-open door. Then she got a heavenly sniff of outdoor air, recognizing at once that this was an unusual opportunity. She walked slowly towards it, guided by smell as well as sound, those muffled high-pitched sounds of tiny animals scurrying through tunnels under the snow pile. She put her nose to the crack of the door, then her whiskers told her it was wide enough for her to squeeze through. Aha! She thought, now's my chance!

She hesitated not a single millisecond before she was heading out the door. Then she leapt to the top step, with no comprehension that her traction would be non-existent. She slid ungracefully off the step and into the soft snow, sinking so deeply that she could barely see out the hole she had made. Her tail, usually her tool for getting out of compromising situations, hardly moved when she tried to flip it around. Her paws moved vigorously but found no purchase, and the

Anne L. Hess
Stillwater, ME

harder she tried, the deeper she went. She could smell the delicious creature just ahead, but this time just beyond her reach since she was blocked by the snow. She thrashed some more, succeeding only in covering herself rather completely with more loose snow. She mewed and cried, she pushed and pulled her paws, she even bit the snow. Not only was she stuck, but now she couldn't be seen! And she was experiencing an entirely new sensation: She was *freezing!* She'd never been cold before. Ever. It was frightening, indeed.

After coming back in the house, Robin did her usual one-lap-around the house to see that all was well. She picked her favorite spot, turned the required four times, and settled in for a nap. It's good to rest, she thought, especially after being in the cold.

Some time passed and Robin awoke to the sound of her human calling "Batcat!" "Batcat, where are you?" No sounds, not even of the miniscule clickings of paws against the maple floors. "Here kitty, kitty!" Robin sat up and sniffed. No smell of Batcat. And her large hairy ears couldn't hear her, either. She and her human looked around in all of Batcat's hidey-holes to no avail. The cat was nowhere to be found, and apparently not even in the house. Where could she be?

Batcat was starting to worry. She didn't know how to get out of this cat-trap, and her humans didn't seem to be looking for her out here. "Hey, you fools, look outside! I'm out here, in the cold!" she tried to shout. Her loudest meow was nearly muted by her icy blanket, and she was very afraid. She was starting to shiver. Her mouth, ears and nose now had snow in them and she could barely breathe.

Her human came out on the air-lock porch looking for Batcat, when she noticed the door that was held open by the snow and ice. Robin was on her heels, and before the human could deduce that Batcat might be outdoors, Robin battered herself through the door and started running around in circles just outside. She paused, ran around some more, paused again and tilted her head just so. She thought she

Anne L. Hess
Stillwater, ME

heard something, a small sound. Where is it? She asked herself. Is it Batcat? Where are you? She shouted in her loudest voice.

The human watched Robin's antics, first thinking her dog was just enjoying romping in the snow. Then she recognized a pattern: Robin was circling, sniffing and moving in a tighter circle. Then Robin plunged her nose into the snow, then lifted her head out and gave a sharp "Here!" bark. Before her human could get there—a mere five feet away—Robin started digging. Fast, furiously she dug. Then she heard the faint meow, and heard a weak heartbeat, and smelled that beloved scent of Batcat!

Her human rushed to the spot, and, without mittens or shoes, she started digging, too. She felt something furry. Slightly warm and soft like a cat's coat. She dug under and around the compacted lump until she could lift it out. Robin kept barking and prancing around, spraying snow this way and that, making sure the human didn't give up on her little buddy.

Human gently dug the remaining snow from around Batcat's torso, legs and head, and lifted her gently out of her snow trap. Batcat was limp, but shivering and mewing almost constantly. "What took you so long?" she thought but couldn't say. The human cradled the cat snugly against her breast, hugging her lovingly, and hurried back in the house with Robin close behind.

Robin wanted to be up close, too, but the human didn't make room for her at first. Robin wouldn't go away, and kept poking her nose around any opening to touch Batcat with her warm, wet nose. The human got a warm blanket and wrapped Batcat in it, then laid her in her cat bed. Batcat looked up at her and rasped a sweet "Thank you!" meow, the best she could do with her limited vocabulary. Robin hovered like a new mother over her newborn pups, nudging Batcat gently and licking her profusely. Now Batcat liked affection, but this amount of dog drool was just too much, no matter

Anne L. Hess
Stillwater, ME

how well-meaning, and she gave a soft hiss. Robin knew it meant to stop, so she just lay down beside Batcat and curled her body around the cat's bed, wrapping her big tail around her for reassurance.

The human fixed the door first thing, chopping the ice and packed snow until the door would close easily. Then she went to the kitchen and made some warm chicken broth and placed a small bowl of it by Batcat. When Robin started to drink it, Batcat hissed again, and began lapping it greedily once Robin backed off. The warmth spread quickly through her small body, and soon she was refreshed and full of mischief again. Even a cat can feel grateful and lucky, which she did.

And she never wanted to go outside again. At least not when the ground was all white. She decided she'd had enough adventures for a lifetime; boredom could have its advantages, too.

***

Thomas Peter Bennett
Bradenton, FL

After the Rain

Gulls hang in the sky
over the river at sunset.

Palm fronds thrum
moist gentle breezes for
a chorus of crickets.

Raindrops keep dropping
from a dock's tin-roof as
a skiff rocks in its cradle.

Marilyn Fleming
Pewaukee, WI

If Not for Winter

It is the morning of the darkest day.
The red dogwood is stripped to the drift
where rabbit tracks gather and end.
Noisy birds are at the withered choke cherries
and the wintered oak whispers utterances
of buried acorns threading in spring.

I brush snow from the cellar door
open to the dank dirt floor
to layers of scattered onion husks
kegs of sand stored carrots
sacks of apples unchanged in months
dull and darkened to a chapped red.
I reach blind into the burlap sack
choose only the firmest
bite into one—watching the
juicy white flesh change colors
the way a dog's bark is brown.

In the end it's all about survival
the things we bury to make it through
the fox holes we find shelter in
and the facades we hide behind
all essential like a goat's second coat
a cast off snake skin or a Mardi Gras
face mask kicked to the curb on Ash Wednesday.

Awarded Honorable Mention in Wisconsin Fellowship of Poets
Triad Contest Nov. 2012
Published 2015 Wisconsin Poets' Calendar

Karyn Lie-Nielsen
Waldoboro, ME

The Iceboat Accident

for Mark McClellan

Water. Soft or hard or ghosting
above itself, he loved it.
Touched it, practiced it,
studied it like an instrument
finding new ways to play it.

Five days before Christmas
when an enormous bowl of it was solid,
he was on top of it, sailing over it
free as the angels from heaven
that lit the treetops
in all the shoreline houses.

Then the bowl broke open.
Water turned on him,
poured over him
spilling him into the freezing boil of it.

It wasn't the devil reaching
from the mud beneath, but water itself
making sandbags of his feet,
weighing his arms with the pure nature of itself,
practicing him like an instrument.

It enveloped him, held him, contained him,
so that all he could see was the clouded
labyrinth of betrayal shifting between him
and the snow-dusted figures along the shore.

Karyn Lie-Nielsen
Waldoboro, ME

He thought of his wife, his children,
the solid anchor of the family table
where they would soon be laying him out
still with the rime of water on his skin,
his friends and family weeping warm salt tears
enough to send him off on his last lone voyage.

Water. He hated it.
When he was out of it,
he would never see it again.

***

Thomas Peter Bennett
Bradenton, FL

Funerary Treasures

With shell and soft body
shellfish alive—
    shell remains after death
    soft body becomes elemental.

Soft bodies entombed
in deep Gulf waters—
    mythic souls in a
    funerary procession of waves.

Shells cast on distant beaches
transfigured by sun—
    resurrected by beachcombers as
    museum treasures.

Joyce M. Pye
Bath, ME

Thanksgiving: South of Memphis

Back home, men store spit-polished
Winchesters in the back pantry,
drape wool jackets on pegs
Pounded by fathers, grampas...
legends who crowd the room
with tales of bucks brought down at dawn.

Children stomp by the door, let sharp
Maine air slip into the kitchen
as they sneak scents of roast goose
and venison bathed in cider, fingers
creeping toward the pumpkin pie

while here on the Natchez Trace
we sip Colombian coffee,
munch gouda-and-sprouts on rye,
watch four wild turkeys peck and strut
on the opposite side of the green

until fading light lures doe
to feed at forest edge.
No wariness, no sound to fear...
the whisper of Choctaw moccasins,
twang of arrow wiped clean.

Laura Platas Scott
Greenville, SC

Simple Rituals

Many, many years ago my wise friend Carole posed an intriguing question as she cuddled my brand-new baby on a cool spring morning.

"So what new Christmas traditions will you start now that you have Ben?"

"I hadn't thought about it, but I love the idea," I said. Eager for all that lay ahead of me in my new role as mother; I was particularly excited to plan for Christmas.

Carole had a great holiday ritual. Every year, a few days before Christmas, her family drove thirty minutes to an old-fashioned movie theater to see *It's a Wonderful Life*, the ageless story of George Bailey, the fictitious town of Bedford Falls, NY and the endearing angel, Clarence, working hard to earn his wings.

The question nagged me. I made a mental list of my own memories—a trek to a Christmas tree lot, baking cookies, setting up the Nativity, the preparations for Noche Buena, singing Christmas carols and visiting Santa, of course, but I wanted something new and fresh to add to that list—a simple ritual that would build sweet family memories over time.

The following November, around the time that Ben was toddling around, I saw a magazine photo of a Christmas tree in the kitchen—my favorite room in the house. I knew right away that I'd found my new ritual. We would have a living room Christmas tree with my husband's antique toy train circling beneath it to continue his family's tradition, but I would add a small Christmas tree in the kitchen—a simple tree without lights—just ribbons and handmade ornaments and old cookie cutters.

I placed a two foot tall artificial tree on a table in the sunny nook of our drafty, tall-ceilinged kitchen. I wanted a live tree, but the little artificial tree had been my father-in-

Laura Platas Scott
Greenville, SC

law's and with his recent passing still fresh on our minds; it was the right tree to launch our new holiday ritual. Ben and I spent an entire happy and messy morning making salt dough, rolling it out and cutting out little stars, trees, gingerbread men and Santas from old cookie cutters I'd used as a child. There was flour on the old wooden floor, on our faces and in our hair. Ben's chubby fingers were caked with dough and the whole time he smiled that sweet, crooked little smile of his. We poked a hole at the top of each doughy ornament—Ben especially loved that part—and then baked them for several hours. That night while Ben slept; I painted the shapes with a quick-drying varnish.

The next day we threaded red and cream plaid ribbon through the hole in each ornament and tied off a loop. Ben stood on a chair, leaning chubby hands on the kitchen table as I helped him hang twenty-four homemade ornaments and the cookie cutters—a reindeer, Santa Claus and gingerbread man made of opaque ruby-red plastic, and a tin star and tree —all circa 1965—donated by my mother.

Carole gave us a little brass bell and we hung it on the tree as well. In the years ahead I rang Carole's little bell at Christmastime to remind me of angels and good deeds and friendship. And I rang it just in case there was an angel out there waiting to earn its wings.

My mom provided the perfect finishing touch to our kitchen tree—an apron she'd made me as a child. White cotton with small red cabbage roses and red rick rack speckled with gold thread, its crescent shape and ruffled edge made it the perfect tree skirt for the kitchen tree. That apron brought back memories of baking bread with my mother in Pittsburgh—back when my love of baby dolls and the kitchen and just about all things domestic was in full bloom. Our kitchen Christmas tree was simple, beautiful and unique.

As the years went by and our family grew, I became a little tree crazy in our house in Georgia—a large tree in the living room for our abundant cache of new and old ornaments,

Laura Platas Scott
Greenville, SC

the kids' holiday crafts from school and below it all, the train scene. There was a second tree in the dining room decorated with only white lights and silver and gold ornaments, a third tree in the basement with only miniature toy ornaments, and the fourth tree—the kitchen tree. I found artificial trees on sale to save money in future Christmases. My youngest son, Sam, wondered why Santa Claus didn't leave presents under every tree in the house. Smart boy—more trees, more bounty.

There may not have been presents under every tree, but every tree was loaded with ornaments. Something about the kitchen Christmas tree charmed my family and friends and I encouraged the steady stream of kitchen-themed ornaments—a tiny rolling pin, a little lady mouse holding a tea bag, a miniature mixer, cinnamon sticks tied with red ribbons and a collection of antique cookie cutters among many, many, many others.

The ritual of a simple, natural tree had evolved into a six foot artificial tree chock full of ornaments, with strands of white twinkly lights and glass candy canes, accented with delightfully realistic garlands of sugary gumdrops and frosted peppermints. The original salt dough ornaments and cookie cutters were in the mix, but not easy to spot. Good thing the tree was artificial; a live tree would have collapsed from the weight of the overzealous splendor.

The fully decked-out kitchen-themed tree was fancy, gaudy, and wildly different than the original kitchen Christmas tree. My child's apron looked lost under the large extravagant tree. One year I tried hanging it from the top—but it didn't look right. I gave up and left it folded in the linen closet.

In a nostalgic mood last Christmas, possibly brought on by the fact that Ben would turn 21 not long after the holiday, I bought a two foot live tree and placed it on a table in a corner of the kitchen of our house in South Carolina. I hung only the brown salt-dough ornaments and original cookie

Laura Platas Scott
Greenville, SC

cutters on its short boughs and tied my child's apron tree skirt around the burlap-covered base. Stepping back to admire the tree, I daydreamed back to a quiet December morning in our tall-ceilinged kitchen in Virginia with my sweet toddler, flour in our hair and on the old wooden floor. The red plastic Santa Claus and reindeer cookie cutters took me back to a small yellow kitchen in Pittsburgh, my mother and I in matching aprons rolling out cookie dough on the grey-speckled Formica table by the window. Simple days; uncluttered and quietly joyful.

That same week, another ritual changed. Ben went with me to the neighborhood tree lot to choose a tree for the living room. I remembered his quiet comment from the previous year as he admired our tree, "It's pretty, but I wish we could decorate live trees, not artificial ones." It was a polite, quiet observation that I'd tucked into my memory.

Ben and I came home with the tallest tree on the lot—a wide, towering 12 foot tall tree cut that very week from land close by in the mountains of western North Carolina. How we got the tree onto the top of my car, up the hill to our street and from the driveway into the living room still makes my eyes widen. Once we'd regained our composure and our breath, we stood back to admire the mammoth tree in our tall-ceilinged living room. Ben smiled his sweet, slightly crooked smile. "Do we have enough ornaments?" I smiled as I glanced towards the kitchen where the simple little home-spun tree sat in the natural light by the French doors. No need for a tall tree in the kitchen or the dining room or the basement. "Why yes, I believe we do." And because we had so many ornaments, the little brass bell that Carole gave me so many years ago would go back to its rightful place, on the little Christmas tree in the corner of the kitchen. But first I would ring it once. Just in case.

Julia Rice
Milwaukee, WI

My Grandpa Had a Spittoon

Daily he left his huge wooden rocker,
walked to the post office and his "club,"
the creamery, where the populace
heard the "Har, har, har" of his laugh.

Retired from farming more years than he farmed,
he spent his love each Christmas.
He sent ten dollars to create our day—
tree and toys, Depression deluxe.

He heard his grandson tried to worship
in both churches—Catholic and Protestant—
for his wife. He told him, "Go to one church"
and with godly wisdom continued,

"Either one, for the family's sake."
At home he disregarded dentures;
he gummed his chaw and laughed.
He roared peace and love across the fields.

Mark D. Biehl
Hales Corners, WI

Flight 107—Economy

Wings tremble
Turbines roar
Buckles snap
The race begins.
The load lifts
And breaths held—
Released.

The privileged few
Drink, dine, lie back.
The others wriggle,
Trying to regain stolen space,
Considering alternatives
To sleep.

Lights return.
Shoes re-discovered.
Bodies unbend.
Trip's end.

***

Summer Palette

Shasta white
Begonia pink
Renegade mustard yellow.
Heron blue
Bull frog green, and
Dragonfly iridescence.

Byron Hoot
Wexford, PA

304. . .

I remember the phone
number of my childhood—
304-292-5996.
I am wanting to call
home today.

　　　　　　　There's a lot
I want to talk about;
I don't even want to begin
with the weather.

　　　　　　　I can still
speak the language though
the meanings have changed
as what I've done has become
my lexicon.

　　　　　　I can hear echoes,
but I don't want to blaspheme,
put words in their mouths
not theirs.

　　　　　　　I'd like to talk
with my dead again
and have the kind of conversation
only they could give. . . .

Charles Boldreghini
Collierville, TN

To a Sparrow

You were but one, one of a flock
That once populated our hedge row
And daily filled the twilight air
With its chirping singsong
As it settled in for each night's sleep.

When I saw you feeding
In our winter-killed lawn
I sought to save you from the hawk
That had already greatly depleted your flock.

Not realizing
That the lawn was perfect camouflage,
I sought to shoo you
To safety in a nearby hedge.
Thus unwittingly I revealed your presence
To the ever watchful eye of the predator.

And when a winged shadow
Appeared on the ground beyond you
I moved quickly
In an attempt to shield you
But the hawk was quicker,
He swooped by me
And clutched you in a taloned claw.

Your death chirp pierced the air
And one small black eye pleaded for help
As the hawk winged away.

Charles Boldreghini
Collierville, TN

The image of that small black eye
Is indelibly imprinted on my mind.
And your death chirp
Will forever resound in my ear.

***

Sally Woolf-Wade
New Harbor, ME

Flood Waters

The river
begins
innocently
as a trickle
then every hour
it laps farther up
the river banks, swells
like a breast filling with milk
groans and heaves itself up on its shoulder
the same way volcanic magma curls
hissing and bubbling over its crest
gulps up the incessant rain
rolls into a shouting roar, a battering ram
like the front ranks of an advancing army.
Workers rush to loosen the cranks
that open the straining levee's gates.
Thundering mountains of muddy water
burst over the helpless fields, fan out
like a drowned woman's hair—
the luckless farmer's sacrifice
to save the cities and homes
swallowed and dragged
downstream.

Jim Ostheimer
Rockport, ME

Asparagus Bed

My crazy brother Tony and I were assigned the task
Of digging the new bed in August heat sixty-
Eight years ago: a veritable trench forty yards long
And three feet deep. The plan had been to bring us together.

We dug and dug, frequently hitting limestone.
A pick was added to extract chunks.
We also found white quartz arrowheads,
And less-common black flint ones.

We became a team after a few days,
Pretending we were trenching in the war.
When accused of not following the straight line,
We responded that the limestone caused us to wander.

At the end of the project, I don't remember our marching
Off singing "Hi-ho, hi-ho, it's off to work we go," but we just
might have,
Because we had done one hell of a job!

***

Sylvia Little-Sweat
Wingate, NC

Violet

Still, beside brown leaves—
shy purple brow of springtime
bearing winter's bruise

Mary Jane Mason
Larchmont, NY

Mrs. Howard

She turned her head this way and that surveying her best hat as it sat atop her mass of grey curls. The old woman peering back at her through the cracked, smoky mirror smiled faintly. Today was going out day and she wanted to look good. *Ladies always dress well when they go out,* she thought to herself as she put her long hat pin with the purple stone, through her black hat—her only hat.

Now she was ready to go and sit in the front window and wait for her niece to come. She wouldn't put on her coat till it was time to leave. She'd already pulled the wheelchair out of the closet and it stood waiting by the front door. That hateful thing—big and heavy like a lumbering hippo, clunky and ugly like an old rusted tractor. She detested having to use it. She wanted to be young and agile again. She wished she could live in the country again with its drooping willows and kindly oaks. She longed to be back in the sundrenched meadows, quiet streets and easy way of life. Here the city was cold, barren, lonely. Everyone living in little boxes stacked up like dog kennels, more crowded than a chicken coup, more noisy than a barnyard. But here she was and that was that. There was no going back, nothing to go back to. Her brother lived here in the city.

When she was indoors she used just the cane. On good days when her knees didn't pain her, she got along without the cane. She'd stop every now and again, rest her thin, wrinkled hand on the back of a chair and see herself running through a field of wild flowers or climbing a mountainside into the clouds. *A person is only as old as they think,* she'd remind herself and then keep on with her chores.

Today she was thinking young. She was anxious to go out and looking forward to choosing a birthday gift for her son. As she wandered through the car parts store in her

Mary Jane Mason
Larchmont, NY

mind, the doorbell jangled her back to the front room. Her niece was here and opening up the wheelchair.

"Are you ready, Auntie?"

"Yes, I'm ready, but did you have any lunch, child?"

"Yes, Auntie, I'm fine." They had the same conversation each time Sally came.

As they moved slowly up the avenue, Mrs. Howard tried to help turn the wheels of the chair. "You just relax and enjoy the scenery, Auntie," Sally would say. "You do the people watching, I'll do the pushing." Ages later, they arrived at the parts store. Mr. Jacobs, the proprietor, welcomed them with his usual, "Hi, how ya doin'?"

What would it be this year? Her son, Chester, had so many tools already. Of course she'd get a tube of Invisible Glove and a new bag of rags, but she wanted something that would light up his eyes. "Mr. Jacobs," she called, "where are your spark plug wrenches?"

"If there are any left, they'll be on the left wall," he called back. "My stock was low and there's not so much call for them any more, Mrs. Howard."

"Oh. Well then, I'll get him a nice box wrench. A medium-sized one will be good."

She scrutinized several of the wrenches, running her fingers over the smooth shaft, putting her thumb in the hole at the end, comparing one to another, feeling their heft. She finally settled on a 5/8 inch and putting it in her lap, wheeled over to the cashier's counter. Carefully, she placed the wrench, the Invisible Glove and the bag of rags on the counter and reached for her pocketbook. Mr. Jacobs totaled up the sale and, slowly, Mrs. Howard counted out the dollars and change. "You'll wrap them up nice and pretty, won't you?"

"Sure thing, Mrs. Howard," Mr. Jacobs said with a smile. He glanced at Sally, standing behind the wheelchair, as he wrapped. Sally, silent, rolled her eyes.

Mrs. Howard double checked the amount of money and

Mary Jane Mason
Larchmont, NY

then placed it on the counter. "Thank you, Mr. Jacobs," she said with a smile. "Sally?"

"Okay, Auntie," Sally said as she turned the wheelchair around to leave. The package remained on the counter and as they left, Mr. Jacobs handed the cash to Sally. They nodded in understanding and smiled.

Out on the street, Mrs. Howard sighed wistfully.

"Maybe they'll find him this year, Auntie. Maybe this year."

***

Diane Colvin Reitz
Winter Park, FL

Falling Away

a cool, wet final rinse in the air...
breathing it in deeply
brushing the face

you hurry to open a window
to breathe in more beginnings
of fall, that changes you

along with the burnt leaves,
the green leaves, the orange gold
leaves—all leaving summer

turning new leaves toward
the direction of quiet, of
a cold wind and silent colors

falling away.

Andrew Badger
Douglasville, GA

A Prodigal

She stands apart from milling crowd,
a garbage bag half-stuffed with clothes
between her feet. Her head hangs low.
Shoulders stooped, she weeps and waits
for her Carolina-bound bus to load.

A yellowed shirtwaist scavenged from
the trash behind a Goodwill store—
too stained to sell—hangs loosely on
her body cov'ring even ankles,
displaying stains from owners past.

The faded tattered red bandanna
tied about her neck catches tears
from trembling chin. Her hand still clutches
both ticket stub for home and crumpled
yellow Western Union plea.

Her days of vivid dreams and sky
high hopes—those points that children use
to gain release from parents' bonds—
had burst and scattered bits on barren
ground awaiting westward winds.

Her mind aswirl with memories of
her mom and dad, of angry words
with spiteful slurs, slamming doors,
sullen wails from hearts that ached—
these more vivid than those dreams.

Andrew Badger
Douglasville, GA

She boards the bus in fearful, fervent
prayer for godly grace, parental
favor, love from those she'd hurt
a thousand miles away on a dusty
Carolina cotton patch.

Her journey ends at a solitary mail box
adorned with Welcome Home balloons
where the arms of a loving family lift
her from the bus to healing balms of home.

***

Rozell Caldwell
Jackson, TN

In Memory of Ernest Brooks
(d. Dec. 2012)

He disappeared in the dead of winter;
The brooks were frozen, the airports almost deserted,
And snow disfigured the public statues, while
The mercury sank into the mouth of the dying day.
What instruments we have agree that
The day of his death was a dark, cold day.
"Earth, receive an honored guest;
Ernest Brooks is laid to rest."

Lorelee L. Sienkowski
Packwaukee, WI

Sweet Mary

Sweet Mary, sit beside me and tell me of your child,
Did he romp and run with others?
Was he always shy and mild?
Did he help solve playmate's squabbles?
Did he start some of his own?
Did he listen to the babble
of the men who sit on thrones?
Did he learn to read from rabbis?
Did he sometimes misbehave?
Did he learn to use the mallet
like his father, tall and grave?
When did he learn his future?
When did he start to teach?
When did you know his end would be?
On a cross just out of reach?
He was so very special;
You must have been so brave,
To mother such a baby
Who would take us through the grave.
I'm glad you had that child;
I'm glad He came to be;
I'm glad to be His child,
I'm glad He still loves me.

Susan Clayton Luton
Austin, TX

Leopold Granger

Leopold Granger teetered, despite the cane supporting him, at the edge of his half-acre garden. His hands hadn't touched the soil in decades, early on because of his frenzy running a company, later because his joints were too stiff for such labor. He stayed at the perimeter, watching and barking orders at Jennings, his full-time gardener, and scowling from the harsh sunlight or some other less fathomable reason. His house, its façade an echo of an antebellum plantation, loomed behind him.

No one could say that Leopold Granger hadn't earned his wealth. After all, he'd started life on Black Monday, 1929, in a sharecropper's shack tilting at the edge of a cotton field. Both he and his mother survived the birthing due only to the grace and knowledge of an elderly neighbor. Under the leaky tin roof, within walls that let in the damp cold of East Texas winters and the wretched heat of its summers, he and his three siblings grew up.

The day Leo turned five he became what his mama called her garden assistant—a fancy title spun from her cleverness with words and a hard-earned eighth grade diploma. When Leo rotated in to garden duty, his brother Raymond rotated out to join their daddy in Mr. Thornton's fields.

In the garden Leo learned about magic. His mother had a more practical explanation for what happened to seeds nestled in dirt and given enough water and light. But Leo wouldn't budge from his belief that only a power beyond the realm of humans could transform objects so inconsequential into violet sugar beets, or watermelon whose pink juiciness punched a hole in summer heat, or emerald stalks of corn that dwarfed everyone but his daddy.

His mother's laugh was the other magical element in the garden. Leo rarely heard it inside walls, except for those of

Susan Clayton Luton
Austin, TX

the dry goods store when she gossiped with other sharecropper wives. But while tending to her vegetable brood, as she called the bounty that ended up on their table, her face looked even younger and laughter rippled from her mouth. Leo found the sound as enchanting as birdsong.

At times his mother would stop working, lift the heavy dark hair from her neck, and gaze at their shack. One day, not long before Leo had to leave for the cotton fields, he asked her why. "Because I still can't believe we live in a house that big," she replied. "It's a palace compared to the one I grew up in." From the stories she'd told, Leo knew her siblings had far outnumbered his own. And he knew how crowded and commotion-filled his house always felt—like being inside the bellows of an accordion. So with her reply an idea was planted in his head: Life can always be worse.

Because of the damage Leo wreaked coming into the world, he was the last child his mother would bear. So she kept him in her garden longer than the others. But finally his daddy insisted, and then life got worse for Leo. In the fields he was handed a sawed-off hoe, told to chop cotton, and was promptly scolded that chopping meant weeding around the young plants, not cutting them down. Months later he was dragging a bag behind him and picking bolls with lacerated hands. When he was older, he had to mop the buds with molasses and arsenic, and his daddy yelled at him if he missed a single one, and the flies swarmed to get at the sweet poisonous mixture—thick clouds of them vying with the mosquitoes he constantly served as a feeding trough.

Before long he divined, at a still tender age, why his daddy seldom talked and never laughed. And he came to understand why Raymond and the twins, Mary and Marlene, slow-boiled with resentment at their fate. As for Leo, he tried hard to find slivers of joy if only for his mother's sake. But this motive was unexpectedly short-lived.

Leopold Granger pivoted on his cane, making Jennings disappear from view. The sun slipped behind a cloud, and in

Susan Clayton Luton
Austin, TX

the gentler light the reds, greens, and purples of his vegetables glimmered like jewels. A memory of his mother flashed through his head, young and sparkle-eyed since death claimed her before she was given a chance to age. *She'd be proud of my vegetable brood,* he thought. But deep down he knew that wasn't true. His mother would have found the enterprise too excessive. And if she were at his side, watching him watch Jennings, she'd have said, "Son, smelling fresh-baked bread isn't the same as eating it."

Reluctant to be inside walls, yet too limp from the moist July heat to stay, Leopold shouted at the old gardener to keep an eye out for aphids then hobbled toward the house. His mother, still fully present in his mind, chided him, "Why on earth would one body need so much space to live in?" But what else could he have done back then with all the money he was accumulating left and right?

At that moment, a yearning to see his mother in the flesh struck so fiercely he nearly tumbled. *I'd give half my fortune to spend a few hours with her,* he thought. He collapsed on a wrought-iron bench and plotted their conversation. He'd explain how he started out as a truck driver at seventeen. How he loved always moving, the highway ribboning out from his rig, because people and relationships were left behind. How he saved up enough to buy his own eighteen-wheeler, then a second, third, and so on, and hired the men to drive them. How money mushroomed, especially as Europe recovered from the insanity of the war. How for years he'd had so much money he passed his spare time figuring out what to do with it. Finally, he'd take her hands so she could feel the absence of scars and callouses on his own. "I vowed at seventeen never to pick cotton again," he'd tell her. "But I own cotton interests in faraway places." And he hoped she would say, "I'm proud of you, Leo. You've done well, Leo." He ran a hand over his head, bald going on thirty years. He hadn't inherited his daddy's hair, which was still thick and wavy when the man's heart stalled at forty-six. He knew his daddy

Susan Clayton Luton
Austin, TX

would be proud of him.

When Leopold walked into the house, the sound of his footsteps bounced off the thick walls, high ceilings, and marble floors. He resented the lonely nature of the sound and wondered whether more oriental carpets might muffle it. Relief bubbled up when he saw Mrs. Whalen at the far end of the kitchen.

"Mr. Granger, can I leave early today?" the housekeeper said as he approached her. "I've finished everything, including your supper, and I need to take my grandson to the doctor."

Leopold scowled. "Again, Mrs. Whalen?" He kept on the lookout for being taken advantage of, and she'd asked the same of him the previous week.

"It's his brother that has the appointment today," the housekeeper said. "The doctor can't figure out the stomach ailment that's plaguing them both. And my daughter's about to lose her job from asking off so much." She lowered her head. "We'd certainly appreciate it, Mr. Granger."

"Go, then," he told her. "But if this keeps on, your daughter needs to make other arrangements."

Mrs. Whalen mumbled her thanks and left.

Now Leopold was alone in the cavernous house. Except for the slight hum of the central air the silence was dense, a vacuum threatening to suck him in. His mother's voice came through the silence. "Do you laugh ever, Leo? Do you ever even *hear* laughter?"

He eased his bony frame into an armchair and thought about the subordinates he'd hired over the years, the men who faked a laugh when he attempted to be clever with words. "Rarely, on both accounts," he answered his mother.

He imagined her shaking her head, uncomprehending, as her eyes traveled around the room. They fell on the enormous paintings—gaudy, but predicted to double in value—and oversized leather furniture and expensive baubles by the dozens. "But where's the warmth of humans, Leo?" she

Susan Clayton Luton
Austin, TX

asked.

He wanted to tell her about Lorraine. How he really had loved the black-haired bookkeeper, almost fifty years ago now, but that she'd slipped through his fingers when he'd been too busy wringing money out of commerce. How, when he'd felt like he could finally take a breath from his work, he realized he was no longer willing to form-fit his waking hours to anyone else's.

"Oh, Leo," his mother said with a sigh, "how did you end up like this? Not expecting to deserve happiness. Are your daddy and me to blame? If so, I'm sorry, son." Her tone went feisty. "But we don't have anything to do with you thinking all this folderol's going to get you somewhere." With that, his mother's presence evaporated, and Leo felt more alone than he had his entire life. He heaved himself up to find a phone. Right now even the voice of Moscowitz, his second in command, would do.

He happened to glance out the French doors, and there was the gardener smiling, bending down stiffly, holding out his arms. A little girl entered the door-framed view and ran to the old man. It was Jennings' great-granddaughter who, he once said, was the spitting image of his daughter and wasn't it odd how genes jumped generations. The thick walls and thick glass blocked out the sounds, but the expressions on the two faces made Leopold's heart clutch.

The silence had reached the point of intolerable when he felt a swat on the back of his leg, just like his mother used to do when she scolded him. "Leo Granger, you do the right thing," he heard her say.

He looked at his watch. In five minutes Jennings would have the tools put away and be driving off with his granddaughter, who picked him up every day. Leopold hobbled faster than usual to his study. With stiff fingers he scrawled out a check to Jennings equal to six months' wages. He hoped he could find the right words when presenting it. Maudlin wasn't his style.

Susan Clayton Luton
Austin, TX

He didn't put away the leather-bound checkbook. Later he would do the same for Mrs. Whalen, maybe a larger amount because of those sick grandchildren. Then, after eating the meal she'd left warming in the oven, he would sit at this desk and plan how to chip away at his fortune. He foresaw it taking a long time.

"Leo, hurry," his mother called from the French doors. "Jennings is leaving. And tomorrow you may see the world differently."

"Coming, Mama," he said, and this time his voice broke the silence.

***

Jim Ostheimer
Rockport, ME

Timeless Defensive Symbols

Timeless defensive symbols appear at once:
the B-52's contrail high in the blue sky,
bald eagle low, ready to pounce.
Timeless defensive symbols.

Bald eagle follows a thermal up high—
small luncheon sought, perhaps an ounce.
B-52 also death for yesterday's eyes.

The contrail will endure after both trounce.
I'm left wanting to say goodbye.
They have both flown or jounced.
Timeless defensive symbols.

Sarah P. Roy
Oakland, ME

Passion

of the yellow sun,
beats down through forest and field,
seeking out the speckled flowers of our earth.
Shadows play around me,
hide and seek,
as I follow the patch-worked
light and dark road
home.

***

Left

Draw me in.
Spit out my bones.
Churn the fat into butter.
Sprinkle left over sugar
onto your grapefruit...
      There,
i am done.

***

Grace

in the beauty of a rose
lies the beetle,
iridescent.

Robert Erickson
Round Pond, ME

The View from the Washington School

I was born in the year 1885
Hard to believe I am still alive
A schoolhouse who has seen it all
Who welcomed the children every fall

I am strong with heavy hewn beams
To carry the load of parents' dreams
Of teaching the young who are so fond
Of living in a village called Round Pond

I saw them all come and go
Harboring and nurturing you know
Through the years good and bad
I was the haven they knew they had

Some good years before World War Two
Not too many pupils left, but a few
Who still tell the stories about me
About who I was, am and want to be

All we must do is look around
The gray hairs can surely be found
They are neighbors right next door
Just ask them, they will tell us more

Leeman, Prior, Poland and Crook
Wilson and Smith could write a book
Cunningham, Osier, Sawyer, just a few
Lailer, Elliot, Fossett...and maybe you

Robert Erickson
Round Pond, ME

The teachers were my life, my blood
Selfless givers who did all they could
To teach the Three R's and more
Preparing us for what was in store

Art and music were always at hand
The Weatherbees formed the Rhythm Band
Geography and English were also taught
And the metal of character was ever wrought

Thanks Mrs. Francis, Mrs. Gifford, Mr. Yates
You have all found peace in heaven's gates
Recently we lost our beloved Thelma Baker
That wonderful teacher has met her Maker

I loved to see the kids have fun
At recess they all went out to run
In the woods they played hide and seek
The boys played Mumbly Peg every week

The president said the war was done
You could hear the bells saying we had won
Mr. Truman spoke from the Capitol dome
Thank God we would see our boys come home

In 1953 my beautiful doors were closed
No one knew what hardship that posed
No laughing, no screaming, no classes
Just blaring silence as each day passes

Empty and alone were true disasters
When along came a fellow, George Masters
I was used as a workshop and that was okay
Since I had workers with me every day

Robert Erickson
Round Pond, ME

Even that had to come to a bitter end
No longer a school and I couldn't pretend
I became a warehouse for years and years
An era lost among my solitary fears

In '07 the firemen said it was my turn
To train the men and that I was to burn
What horror to think of going up in flame
With nothing left but a remembered name

One day along came the wonderful three
Smith, Meyer and Jansen to love and save me
Later came two, Wright and Cleaves
All of them had rolled up their sleeves

Morton, Herndon, Hixon and Coombs
Dolan also worked to brighten my rooms
Sand and paint, ladders, hammers and nails
All the junk was thrown out in big pails

In June please come and look at me
I am a new, happy schoolhouse you see
My children are back and parents will go
Thank you Round Pond, thank you so

***

A Moment in Time

A moment in time is gone.
All my "have to's" are done.
Another cycle of life is past.
How many more while I last?

Rebecca Recor
Round Pond, ME

The Rings

"They have to be here!" I muttered to myself as I plunged my bare arm into another twenty gallon plastic bucket filled with slurry. My fingers squeezed handfuls of taupe-colored ooze at each level, groping their way to the bottom until the chilly mixture of clay and water engulfed my entire arm. "Would a small metal object sink to the bottom or hang suspended near the top with the discarded material from last night's pottery class?" I wondered. Not knowing the answer, my aching fingers kept filtering the sludge. Only six more buckets to check.

I distinctly remembered the anticipation I'd felt the night before at pottery class as I threw a three pound ball of clay onto a thick bat of the pottery wheel. Squeezing a wet sponge onto the clay, I depressed the foot pedal and hunched over to begin the dance of centering the clay. Totally focused, I brought the clay to life, feeling my energy control the clay as it flowed up and down, up and down. I was about to dig my shortnailed thumbs into the spinning mound to create a well when I felt something hard on my left hand. My concentration splintered as I realized it was my wedding rings. I had forgotten to remove them before leaving home. The grit in the clay would mar the finish, so they had to come off. Irritated by the interruption, I stopped the wheel. I easily slipped the curved golden bands off my finger, but my hands were so slimy that I couldn't tuck the rings into my jeans' pocket. Not wanting to take the time to wash my hands thoroughly, I did the next best thing. I carefully placed the rings on a clean dry corner of the ledge connected to my wheel.

Returning to the clay, I tried to pick up the rhythm again, but I was no longer in the zone. The walls of my pot rose with each pull, but as I made the transition from inside to outside pressure to form the neck of the vase, I pushed just a bit too

Rebecca Recor
Round Pond, ME

hard. The wall wobbled then the entire vessel collapsed into an amorphous blob. Groaning, I straightened my back, rolled my shoulders, scraped the clay off the bat, and dumped the stillborn creation onto my slush pile. I slammed another wedged ball of clay onto the bat and started over. Without distractions this time, I guided the clay into the form I'd envisioned. By the end of the evening, I'd created a trio of vases of different heights but with the same fluid lines. "A good night's work," I smiled as I transferred them to the drying shelf.

As usual, I'd ignored the first two calls to start cleanup because I wanted to finish the project at hand. Scrambling to clean up my station when most of the others were already walking out the door, I scraped my clay trimmings into the water bucket, washed down my wheel, cleaned my tools, and swept around my station. Richard, the instructor, stood with his hand on the light switch by the door as I finished up, obviously anxious to leave. I promised to start my cleanup earlier next week.

It wasn't until I was getting ready for school the next day that I couldn't find my rings. I froze, realizing that I must have left them at pottery class. There was no time to retrieve them before school, but I called during my morning break and the secretary promised to look for me. "Please be there," I thought to myself. "Don't let it happen again." Good jewelry and I don't get along. The gold ring with the amethyst flower petals my parents had given me for my sixteenth birthday, the sandstone ring from a Colorado vacation, the silver dogwood pin my first boyfriend Van Edington had given me when he returned from his Boy Scout Jamboree in Virginia, my Murphy High School class ring had all mysteriously disappeared from my possession. The missing vintage gold pendant Dave had given me as a wedding present didn't really count as my fault as it was stolen from the jeweler who was replacing the stones. But it couldn't happen this time. Not my wedding rings. The school day passed in a blur.

Rebecca Recor
Round Pond, ME

No one answered my call after school so I drove straight to the Mt. Prospect Park District building. No jewelry had been turned into the Lost and Found by the night custodian or from daytime classes, but I raced to the pottery studio to check for myself. I found nothing on the floor, or the shelves, or on my wheel, yet the rings had to be somewhere. Objects don't cease to exist. I tried to reconstruct my actions of the night before. I'd carefully placed the rings on the ledge surrounding my pottery wheel, but maybe they'd gotten mixed in with my slush pile and been scraped into the big plastic buckets used to reconstitute the used clay. Clenching my teeth, I pushed up my sleeve and began my search. Going through the messy process, I wondered why this always happened to me. Did I have a jewelry-craving dwarf following me around swiping my valuables when I wasn't looking? Was my alter ego stashing glittery objects in a secret cache like a magpie? Was I subconsciously destroying symbols of important milestones of my life? I didn't think so, but there had to be some reason my jewelry disappeared much more often than other people's.

After checking every bucket, every ledge, every sink drain, every nook and cranny of the studio, and leaving my name and phone number in the office in case it was turned in, I headed home. I would have to tell my husband that I had lost my wedding rings.

Dave took the news more calmly than I expected. He didn't scream or yell or heap burning oil on my head. He could probably tell that I was feeling guilty enough without that. He accompanied me back to the Park District for another fruitless search and then announced that he would call the jeweler in the morning to see if the same ring was still available. I offered to pay for it, but he said it was the husband's responsibility. We ended up splitting the cost. When the rings came in, they looked the same: they had the familiar offset curves so they would fit smoothly on my finger and we arranged for the engagement ring to be soldered to the

Rebecca Recor
Round Pond, ME

wedding band so they wouldn't separate. It felt good to have rings back on my hand and they stayed there for many years. Yet the new diamond never seemed quite as bright as the original, not as perfect in shape, and it was a constant reminder of my carelessness. There had been that moment when I'd made a choice not to put the rings in a safe place. I'd been so focused on my hobby, creating the perfect pot out of clay, that I had sacrificed the symbols of my marriage. If there was more to be read into my actions than that, I chose not to think about it.

Ten years later Dave died. When I eventually removed the replacement rings from my finger, I gave some thought to what had happened to the original rings. Had someone slyly walked off with them, had they been washed through the plumbing system out into the depths of Lake Michigan, or had they somehow ended up wedged into clay for someone else's more-valuable-than-expected piece of pottery?

***

Anne W. Hammond
Woolwich, ME

Midwinter Dawn

Inside a cloud,
Outlines weld.
Mist suffuses the air,
Surface shifts underground veil,
Panorama turns gray.
Dawn arrives, outlines grow:
Tree line, bay line,
The copses of eastern pines, leafless trees.
Time slips away
The whole is one.

Gerry Di Gesu
West Chatham, MA

Spring Day

Dangling prisms refract comets of color and hope
across stark walls of my kitchen and heart

The cat stalks a rabbit which becomes
a frozen statue hidden behind red tulips

Squirrels and jays battle at the feeder

The phone—
death of a friend, prayers for my daughter,
my husband's soft voice

Mail—
hope for a cancer patient, birth of a baby

I write—letters, essays, poems

Late rays of sun slant through the window
and form a golden orb of promise
enveloping daffodils in a green bowl

Light rests on forsythia reaching for joy
from a vase in a corner of the room

This beauty existed last spring but was unseen

Today I taste peace.

Carol Leavitt Altieri
Madison, CT

Other-Worldly Creatures in an Acoustic Storm

> *For thou didst cast me into the deep,*
> *Into the heart of the seas,*
> *And the flood was round about me;*
> *All thy waves and billows passed over me.*
> —Jonah 2:3

Our ship rolls roughly in ocean swells.
Off the coast of the Pacific Ocean
humpbacks and sperm whales
with deep set eyes cavort in pods.
Bubbles flow from blow holes.
In the nurturing bath of the sea, dorsal fins knife
through water as pectoral fins glide past.
Announcing their positions,
humpbacks sing arias, sperm-whales
click dialects and Pacific grays drum
poundings of chirp-like whistles.

At Navy's Submarine Surveillance,
the Navy increases sonar intensity until it ricochets
off the ocean floor.
One pod of whales, pups to elders cringe
close to shore, mill in circles in one direction
and then another,
become trapped in a cove.
All panic as they slap flukes against the water.

In every ocean an acoustic storm,
in every continent sonar-
depth charges on whales and dolphins leave
hundreds stranded en masse
in shallow waters, like castaways.

Carol Leavitt Altieri
Madison, CT

Hearing and navigation damaged,
unable to vocalize they can't locate mates.
A deaf whale is a dead whale!
Whale bellies lodge and twist in sand.
Devotees pour ocean water over them
and struggle to push them back. Sharks regroup.

***

Marilyn Fleming
Pewaukee, WI

Fade to White

the way snow blankets a city—
streets and alleys—sidewalks
bus stops disappear in whiteout
—the same way a farmer walks in
overalls pant legs powder coated
swinging a pail of lime tossing
handfuls on walls gutters and
walkways—dark stains fade to white—
winter livestock huddle in the
barnyard snorting puffs of steam
snow covers the manure pile
—wisps of heat vapor rise

lies are like that—wearing city clothes
a false dawn whitewashed—spilled salt
a pinch tossed over my left shoulder
at the black devil lurking there

Published Lake City Poets online Anthology Issue 13
January 2015

Noelle F. Carle
Bristow, OK

Emily in the Moonlight

This is how I see you
in the moonlight on the ice.
Snow glitters, an earthly starry host
on this fine and flawless night.
Wind catches your laughter,
far flung into the darkness.

You, blissful too,
raise your arms and lie down
in the shadows far from shore.
The snowy stars your bed.
Wounded angel, weary heart.
Solace sure—here with you
in the moonlight
on the ice.

***

Sally Belenardo
Branford, CT

Long Island Sound

Breezes crank out hurdy-gurdy music
and pull the ropes of steeple bells
as rigging clanks and clangs
against aluminum masts
of boats moored at marina,
the sound calling sailors
to their worship of the water.

Donna DeLeo Bruno
Bristol, RI

The Currency of Words

Words are my currency. I spend them lavishly when describing a scene or experience; I do not hoard them stingily or use them sparingly. When speaking, I caress them with my tongue; their mellifluous sound sweetens everything I say. Even as a small child, I have always appreciated the beauty of words. Since my grandparents were Italian, I relished their pronunciation with the rolling "r". What more exquisite way to express their love for me than addressing me with the adoring term "Carina" (dearest one). I grew up also realizing the power of words, acutely aware of their ability to immediately evoke intense emotions—both positive and negative. One might say, "Well, naturally, you are a writer who works with words every day—stringing them together in phrases and sentences, adept at using transition expressions (in addition, nevertheless, consequently, finally), strategically building to logical conclusions in expository essays or employing a clever turn-of-phrase to make a point." Rhythm, particularly staccato, as well as parallelism are also effective: "To strive, to seek, to find, and not to yield." (Alfred Lord Tennyson).

But words are not the currency of only the writer. They are tools each of us employs every day to communicate our thoughts, our feelings, our ideas, our very selves. Woe to him who uses them carelessly or thoughtlessly. We can all relate to impulsively speaking in anger or impatience, only to rue that once they are released, we cannot take them back. Well-known is the truism, "The pen is mightier than the sword." This fact emphasizes the permanence of words, their enduring effect to convince, sway, capture the minds and hearts of those upon whose ears they fall. In this way they have a powerful influence on the listeners. Hitler's rhetoric is the most heinous example of their impact on the mass audience and

Donna DeLeo Bruno
Bristol, RI

their ability to accomplish dire results. On the other hand, in the dramatic works of William Shakespeare, we are moved by the "Bard's" exquisite use of words to convey the intensity of human emotions. One example is in the famous balcony scene with Juliet resting her chin upon her hand, reminiscing about her first encounter with Romeo at the Capulet ball. She has fallen instantly and passionately in love. Hidden in the dense garden foliage below, Romeo overhears her confession of love for him and this sweetest line of iambic pentameter captures his mutual attraction: "Oh, that I might be a glove upon that hand that I might touch that cheek!"

Separate and apart from writers like myself, tyrannical despots like Adolph Hitler, and genius playwrights like William Shakespeare, our mundane use of words in everyday conversations has the same power to ignite, to persuade, to convince, and—yes—to hurt. Although we may not have the talent or imagination of the professional writer or orator, our personal and deliberate selection of words does indeed have the power to touch others keenly. Let us be cognizant of their awesome effect and utilize them wisely, compassionately, and lovingly.

***

Robert Erickson
Round Pond, ME

Old

When we are long of tooth
And white of hair
Why is it such a truth
That our women are so fair

Jackie Ascrizzi
Montville, ME

Landscape Changes

Oh, how the landscape has changed,
marsh marigold lost to a drain pipe,
arching alders downed by ice,
apple branch lopped off by a windstorm.
Beavers did their work before tucking
in for winter, grew the frog pond,
shallowed the stream to spread into
the woods, made a clearing on
the hill for ladyslippers.
The house finally got painted, that
grey-green of the one toward
town. The compost abandoned.
Raspberries gone to bramble.
Lost, downed, lopped, shallowed,
abandoned, bramble.
Oh, how the landscape has changed.

***

The Colors of Winter

Raven swoops down over the white landscape,
settling on a field of snow, edged with
dark tree trunks and white birch,
mauve and silver spilling across distant mountains.
Brown leaves skitter over frozen ponds,
deep green hemlock standing guard along the shore.
The colors of winter envelop the world.
Stark and soft, like a broken heart.
Stunning and everyday, like losing love.
Magical and hard, like hopes, like dreams.

Janice Babcock
Wauwatosa, WI

Mother Karmela,
Prioress of St. Joseph Monastery in Croatia

Foundress, educator, leader, wise woman
Gifts of guidance in lay and spiritual areas

Consultant sought by people both powerful and ordinary
     folk
Constrained within space, her help knew no boundaries

Strong woman in the face of direct attack
Fast action on short notice

Used creative survival skills
Secured protection for her community

Resilience to rise above the ashes of war
A true phoenix

Ability to dream, design, plan and execute
Built brick by brick a safe and secure domicile

Showed compassion, love, and protection
Devoted to her cause, she led by example

Gave inspiration to others
Forgiveness from her heart to begin again

She was a treasure
Blessed with vision

Respected by all
A woman of achievement

Janice Babcock
Wauwatosa, WI

Alive with zeal
She touched many lives

Mother Karmela, a wise woman

This earthly red rose is now a heavenly jewel!

***

Charles Van Buren
Brunswick, GA

Time

The little bird tapped at my window,
  reminding me of the Raven,
and just like old Edgar Allen,
  I could find myself no haven.

The tormented mind travels many roads,
  mostly where it has been before,
and wishes it had the power,
  to travel those roads once more.

Maybe Einstein was right all along,
  time is a relative thing,
yesterday probably never was,
  and tomorrow a solution will bring.

But, suppose tomorrow never comes,
  then what of yesterday?
are both endless strands of time,
  to be savored another day?

Amy Lavin Liston
Portland, ME

Landscape

Take down the sun
lest it drip molten yellow
through the sky.

Sky-blue sky, pure, untrue,
overflies unnerving schemes of land,
veers toward its vanishing point.

A river is hardly ever blue.
At its reaches, a hint of the lapsing,
scumbled sea.

Look for grass in a crowd
of low brushstrokes
trying to be green.

About red: it bleeds
as we have bled, have been bled.

We are left with paler things—
clouds, distant animals.

Juliana L'Heureux
Topsham, ME

A Meaningful End to the Vietnam Era

Dedicate some of your life to others.
Your dedication will not be a sacrifice.
It will be an exhilarating experience,
because it is an intense effort applied toward
a meaningful end.
　　　　　　　　　　　　　　　　—Dr. Tom Dooley

In my formative years, when I first started thinking about becoming a nurse, my decision was influenced a great deal by the heroic work of an inspired physician named Tom Dooley, M.D. During the 1950s and early 1960s, Dr. Dooley's humanitarian work in Vietnam and Laos was documented in his autobiographical accounts. He wrote several books about his work to bring western medical and obstetrical sciences into the people living in the jungles of Southeast Asia, known then as French Indo China.

Dr. Dooley died in 1963, when he was only 34 years old, from melanoma.

Fast forward only 12 years, to 1975, in Subic Bay, Philippines. My family was living in Subic Bay in the 1970s when my husband was on Naval duty there.

While immersed in the midst of thousands of Vietnamese refugees, I thought about how many of them were likely from families who had been helped by Dr. Dooley.

When reading Dr. Dooley's books as an impressionable teenager, I certainly had no idea that one day I might be face-to-face with the people he had been helping in Vietnam. Later, I thought sadly about how much work he left behind. As a matter of fact, I asked myself whether any of his humanitarian efforts had made a difference in the lives of Vietnamese people.

In 1975, I was on a pontoon boat in Subic Bay, in the

Juliana L'Heureux
Topsham, ME

Philippines, literally face-to-face with hundreds of desperate Vietnamese refugees who were on board, being transported by the US Navy. Each of them was visibly despondent and desperate. They were experiencing a humanitarian relocation. To a person, they were fleeing the fall of their crumbling nation to the victorious People's Republic of Vietnam. It was the end of the Vietnam War and the US was pulling out, fast.

Although most people think about the history of the Vietnam conflict and the war as being a part of the 1960s, the US involvement began in the middle 1950s and extended well beyond the April 30, 1975 fall of Saigon. In fact, military nurses arrived in Vietnam in April 1956, for the purpose of training the Vietnamese nationals about how to provide care for victims of the country's civil war. Before long, the US military nurses, most of them serving with the Army and Air Force, were already caring for American battlefield casualties, when the war accelerated.

In April of 1975, the Vietnam War was going very badly. In spite of the impending collapse of South Vietnam's government in the months before the war ended, American military and their families, who were living on military bases in the Philippines, at Clark Air Base and Subic Bay Naval Station, were ill prepared for the humanitarian crises that unfolded, after April 30, 1975, when Saigon fell.

As a result, there was little advanced warning or any training for the humanitarian crises we witnessed, when many thousands of Vietnamese refugees arrived in Subic. When the iconic helicopter was lifting the refugees off the roof of the US embassy in Saigon, most of those who survived wound up in hastily created Philippine camps. An urgent call for help by the International Red Cross mobilized the military families living in the Philippines. We responded to the humanitarian crises after the Vietnam People's Army or VPA (a.k.a. Viet Cong) occupied Saigon, renaming it Ho Chi Ming City, to honor their Northern Vietnamese leader.

Distressed Vietnamese refugees arrived in the Philippines

Juliana L'Heureux
Topsham, ME

around the clock. Many of them piled on like logs on a forestry truck inside of US military transport airplanes to fly the relatively short distance from the besieged Saigon airport to the Naval Air Station Cubi Point and Clark Air Force Base.

Unfortunately, there were uncounted numbers who hung on to practically anything that floated across the South China Sea. Tragically, the mortalities among those lost at sea will never be known. Many found passage on cargo ships, living as family units in metal shipping containers.

I boarded one of the refugee ships with a US Navy physician. We were taking a count of how many of the passengers might have tuberculosis. My nursing care consisted of counting those who were considered to be "sick."

"Who is sick on this boat," we asked? Although French was the language they were most comfortable speaking, the refugees responded to the word "sick." A few of the refugees began to point out people among them who they identified as being "sick."

Many boat refugees who arrived in Subic were found living in cargo bins. They were overwhelmingly young adults who appeared to be middle class Vietnamese. Their social class notwithstanding, they were people without a country. Their grief was evident, because they knew it was impossible for them to return to their homeland.

One young girl was crying uncontrollably because her dog was left behind. I also saw a few American ex-servicemen who had likely stayed in Vietnam after their discharge from the military, but were now among the refugees.

Participating in this humanitarian rescue effort brought to mind the images of the people described by Dr. Dooley, in his autobiographical reports. Surely, some of his patients were probably among those who the Americans were helping to evacuate from their war ravaged country. Sadly, I recall wondering how many of Dooley's patients were, in fact, among those we had left behind?

I suspect many of those who were left behind were con-

Juliana L'Heureux
Topsham, ME

sidered to be sympathetic to Americans and, thereby, forced to attend reeducation camps, after the war ended.

Refugees arrived by the thousands to Naval Air Station Cubi Point. After landing, they were transported by trucks and buses to Subic Bay. Pontoon boats waited for them to board, to be moved and quarantined on Grande Island. This tiny shelter was really a beautiful park and recreation site in Subic Bay. Grande Island was where American military families enjoyed picnics, hiking and camping while living on the busy Navy base. As a recreational respite for the base personnel, the island's hiking trails would lead walkers to the remains of a few World War II sand block fortresses, built by the Japanese to defend Luzon Island during the occupation.

Vietnamese refugees were herded by the thousands into quickly erected shelters on this beautiful piece of property, dotted with austere structural relics of World War II.

Many didn't even have the benefit of receiving any shelter, at all. In fact, so many refugees were herded together on Grande Island, it became impossible to count them. Their population density was too thick to arrange for a population count. As a result, the base recreation facilities provided horses from the Special Services' stables, to the few who could ride them, to use as transportation on Grande Island, while a population census could be organized.

Part of our job as volunteers was to pass out cans of soda and bologna sandwiches to every refugee, but this effort was absolutely useless. The Subic Bay water was quickly littered with white bread, floating like a carpet of white alien fungi. We didn't understand, at the time, the cultural shock of giving the Vietnamese food to eat with their fingers. Obviously, sandwiches are not served with any utensils. Moreover, few of the refugees could tolerate eating white bread. As for the bologna....well, it was a strange flavor and texture, to say the least. So, they threw the sandwiches away.

Instead, what the refugees yearned to eat was rice. Many even carried small bags of rice on their person on their ardu-

Juliana L'Heureux
Topsham, ME

ous journey.

Looking back on this refugee relief, I realized how my minimal contribution as a Navy wife, at the time, was more or less a side bar when compared to the experiences of the Vietnam War's military nurses. They cared for the physically and mentally wounded military when trauma care was most needed. They helped to provide medical treatment, mental health and drug rehabilitation care during the war.

One of the Maine nurses who served in Vietnam was Beth Clark. She wrote an article for the *Bangor Daily News*, on November 28, 2003, describing some of her war experiences. "We were the nurses of the 12th Evacuation Hospital. We were stationed in Cu Chi, Vietnam, a hellhole to all who knew it. I was an operating room nurse and part of the advance team that set up the 12th Evac." (The 12th Evacuation Hospital was established in Cu Chi, along Highway 1 on December 1, 1966 in support of the 25th Infantry Division and remained on site until its deactivation on December 15, 1970. http://www.illyria.com/evacs.html#12th).

"A handful of other nurses and I first served with the 7th Surgical Hospital, more properly listed as the 7th Mobile Army Surgical Hospital. We called it Surg, pronounced 'surge,' but you called it M*A*S*H. The operating rooms were, of course, where we performed surgery on wounded men. We could handle seven surgeries at once at the 12th Evac. That sounds pretty good until you realize that we might take in well over 200 wounded during a single battle. Still, it was better than our capability at the 7th Surg, where we could only operate on three or sometimes four soldiers at one time."

Clark was among the 265,000 women who served in Vietnam. She later became one of the women who helped inspire the Vietnam War Women's Memorial, dedicated in 1993, in Washington D.C.

Over the decades, since these events happened, I've frequently thought about the dire circumstances faced by the

Juliana L'Heureux
Topsham, ME

thousands of frantic Vietnamese refugees. In a way, it was a blessing to realize that Dr. Dooley didn't live to witness the carnage, whereby his work to establish jungle clinics was swept away by the victorious Viet Cong Army.

Quite unexpectedly, there was a chance episode of closure to the experience we left behind when we returned home from three years living in the Philippines. It was exhilarating to hear from one young man, over 30 years later, who happened to be involved in a serendipitous conversation with my husband. While we were living and working in Maine, my husband came home with a story to finally bring closure to the experiences I reminisced about. In a work project, he'd been on the telephone speaking with a young man in Texas, when the chit-chat turned to the inevitable, "So, where are you originally from?" question. It turned out, the young man on the telephone was living in Texas, but his family had been among the refugees who were housed on Grande Island, in Subic Bay, during the 1975, emergency evacuation of Saigon.

As a matter of fact, the young unidentified Vietnamese man broke down in expressive gratitude to those of us who he never knew, but who had helped his family to escape from the Viet Cong, after the Vietnam War ended.

Dr. Dooley's quote certainly came full circle to me with the young Texas man's story. It seemed as though the physician's spirit was, somehow, influencing the telephone conversation. Quite coincidentally, we heard from a meaningful end, because the humanitarian work we did was acknowledged and became absolutely exhilarating.

Americans visiting Vietnam today are welcomed with enthusiasm. Frankly, when my husband and I visited Vietnam in 2011, we experienced friendship, without animosity, towards Americans. It was like the people had organized our homecoming.

It certainly seems like the hard working and prospering Vietnamese people have also achieved a meaningful end to

Juliana L'Heureux
Topsham, ME

their era of war and turmoil.

After working as a nurse for most of my professional career, I am proud to say I was inspired by Dr. Dooley's dedication and sacrifice.

Responding to the Vietnamese refugee humanitarian crises in the Philippines was a rare nursing opportunity. I participated in a sad historic event, while, also, being part of helping to provide unknown thousands of people with the opportunity to start new lives.

***

Noelle F. Carle
Bristow, OK

February Waning

This gritty winter against which we chafe
    this leaden sky pressing
    these gusty fingers of ice
    and darkened sun.

How we shrink and murmur
    at so long and so cruel a cold,
    as bound, we wait, and sigh, and wonder.

At last, when we had most
    doubted but strongest hoped—
    is yielded up a precious, shimmering
    lustrous pearl of a day.

Lilli Buck
Bristol, VA

"Freedom" Is a Holy Word

Oh, "freedom" is a holy word,
A holy word like "peace,"
When all the chains are broken,
And all the guns have ceased.

Oh, "freedom" is a holy word,
A holy word like "love,"
Which is born in every mother's heart,
And comes from God above.

Oh, "freedom" is a holy word,
A holy word like "truth,"
When all lying is forsaken,
And all vows are made forsooth.

Oh, "freedom" is a holy word,
A holy word like "light,"
When dawn shines on the ocean waves,
And flocks of birds take flight.

Oh, "freedom" is a holy word,
A holy word like "home,"
When you're happy in your little place,
And never long to roam.

Oh, "freedom" is a holy word,
A holy word like "forgive,"
When vengeance is not taken,
And sinners choose to live.

Lilli Buck
Bristol, VA

Oh, "freedom" is a holy word,
A holy word like "healed,"
When the lame get up and walk,
And God's power is revealed.

Oh, "freedom" is a holy word,
A holy word like "sight,"
When the blind man, long in darkness,
First beholds the shining light.

Oh, "freedom" is a holy word,
A holy word like "blessed,"
When you're weary from your labors,
And Jesus gives you rest.

Oh, "freedom" is a holy word,
A holy word like "saved,"
When Jesus comes into your heart,
And takes your sins away.

Oh, "freedom" is a holy word,
A holy word like "prayer,"
When you go within and seek the Lord,
And find Him waiting there.

Oh, "freedom" is a holy word,
A holy word like "silence,"
When unkind words are left unspoken,
Which could have led to violence.

Oh, "freedom" is a holy word,
A holy word like "lowly,"
When you walk humbly with your God,
And with the Spirit Holy.

Lilli Buck
Bristol, VA

Oh, "freedom" is a holy word,
So beautiful to hear.
It falls like tender music
In the hollow of your ear.

Oh, "freedom" is a holy word,
When spoken by the tongue,
Like when all the birds are singing,
And the wedding bells are rung.

But "freedom" is a holy word
That's wasted on the free,
Who have never known what bondage is,
Or been a slave like me,

Who have never stood on an auction block
In manacles and chains,
To be sold like beasts of burden,
To work the fields in pain.

Then you'd get up every morning
And thank God that you are free,
For "thank you" is a holy word,
Like "love" or "liberty."

Then you'd get up every morning
And sing to God His praise,
For "Praise the Lord" are holy words,
By which the soul is raised.

Then you'd serve the Lord with gladness,
To thank Him for your liberty,
For "service" is a holy word,
When spoken by the free.

Lilli Buck
Bristol, VA

"Freedom" is the word I heard
When I got up today.
When I heard I had my freedom,
I fell down on my knees to pray

And I wept with joy that I was free,
And thanked the Lord so dear,
For "freedom" is the holiest word
That any slave can hear.

And I thought I heard the angels singing
Like when Jesus Christ was born.
I thought I heard their trumpets ringing
As they did on Christmas morn.

And I heard the slaves all singing,
Shouting, clapping in the sun,
And the words they sang were "Freedom,
Freedom now for everyone."

***

Irene Zimmerman
Greenfield, WI

In October

Driving before dawn
past fields sleeping in
after yesterday's performance,
I replay their symphonies of sumac,
choruses of cornfields
until at last—in the east—
a hint of arriving trumpets.

Patricia Lynne Janke
Wauwatosa, WI

Crystals

Time sparkling in seconds
Dreaming in precious hues
Tinkling vibrations
Neurons bursting clues

Feel joy to your fingertips
Capture smiles with your eyes
Save laughter in your heart
Remember each and every sigh

Fill memory with holiday scents
Nostrils with pine purism
Sing out traditional hymns
Shaking gently glassy prisms

Never take for granted
Hours spent with love
Fleeting moments rush by
Sent from heaven above

***

Susan Gerry
Friendship, ME

Osprey

Hungry osprey
　　　rests on a bowsprit
watching the lunch menu
　　　swim by.

Helen Gioulis
Philadelphia, PA

From Away

I could tell that fishing was in his blood just by the way he stood with his long skinny legs firmly planted in the shallows. His steely eyes methodically scanned the pond's surface as he focused on the activity of the flies, while he waited patiently for the big one to come his way. Nothing distracted him, neither the dragonflies that skimmed the water nor the loon that surfaced after a long dive. Then, almost presciently, he turned his head to the right just as a small bass jumped to catch a fly. He didn't waste his energy going after this small fry because he knew instinctively, that a real meal would be coming soon.

I watched him for a few minutes from behind the sliding glass door, mesmerized by his Zen-like intensity and stillness of being. I walked away for just a minute to get my shoes, but when I returned he was gone. I stepped onto the deck, hoping to see him by the bend in the shoreline, but he had vanished.

I didn't intend to disturb his solitude or his fishing. I just wanted to get a better look at him. Clearly, he didn't want some woman disrupting his silence or sharing his perfect fishing spot where the water was warm and a bit weedy. I had jarred his reverie, and it just didn't sit right with him. He was a real Mainer, born and bred in these parts. I was "from away" as they say in Maine, and he was wary of strangers who might try to get too close.

It was my first season on Biscay Pond, a five mile long expanse of water, which anywhere else would have been called a lake. Since there were both ponds and lakes in the region, I assumed size was the determining factor. Just to satisfy my curiosity, I asked a few people local to the area, but soon realized by the blank stares and odd looks, that there was no logical explanation. It's just the way things are in mid-coast Maine.

Helen Gioulis
Philadelphia, PA

It must have been the oddity of my questions that prompted the usually reserved Mainers to ask where I was from, and what had brought me to the area. When I replied that I was a Philadelphian, who had grown up near Boston, they responded with a nod. When I mentioned that I had friends who summered in Maine, another singular nod. I presumed they were nods of semi-approval, but then again, maybe not. I could almost hear them say, "At least, she's not from New York." As a general statement they aren't fond of New Yorkers, an animosity that probably stems from the rivalry between the Red Sox and Yankees. One thing is certain; however, Mainers aren't keen on bossy types whether home grown or from away.

True to their reputation, they tend to keep their distance. For them friendship is earned in small sips, not freely poured. They respect hard work and quietly give high scores of approval to those willing to get their hands dirty. When the plumber was loading his tools in his truck after repairing my problematic sink, he noticed that I was dragging a fifty pound bag of mulch. With a slight smile and a bit of a twinkle in his eyes he asked if I had come to Maine to work. When I replied that "gardening was my savage amusement," he laughed heartily, helped me with the unwieldy bag, then got into his truck. Now, whenever I see him, he always asks how my garden is coming along and smiles.

My neighbors noticed my wave of hello as I drove by, that I remembered the names of the shopkeepers, and that I praised the workmanship of the local carpenters and craftsmen. They imperceptibly absorbed my actions into an opinion. In time, and without fan fare, they extended genuine friendship. I knew the initial skepticism had turned into acceptance when Betsy, "from across the pond," as she likes to say, called my caretaker to report suspicious lights at my house. It was April, and she knew that I didn't open for the season until mid May. Or the first time Alfred, who mows my

Helen Gioulis
Philadelphia, PA

lawn, knocked on my door and yelled "H..e..l..e..n" (like it was a multisyllabic word). "Good to see ya!" he said with a grin, as I opened the door to him and to another season by the pond. It's just the way things are in mid-coast Maine.

I remember the soggy June afternoon when the realtor with the stunning blue eyes showed me the house for the first time. Green in every hue had enveloped the property. Hemlock branches with their languid curves rested on empty window boxes, a lilac branch sprawled across the front door, and a mat of forsythia leaves blocked the view from the kitchen window. Bats were peacefully ensconced, weeds were in their glory, a resident black snake was basking on the stoop, and the beaver clan was building a sprawling lodge. The gardeners, the caretakers and the former owner were all gone. There was no one to prune, trim or care—no one to jar the silence with laughter. Nature had reclaimed the land and desolation the house.

Yet, the gently rolling land flowing gracefully to the water was unmistakably beautiful. It had the soft curves of a reclining woman sleeping contentedly by her beloved. I heard a gentle whisper in my ear, "Sit beside me and feel my magic." My logic said, "Are you crazy?" My heart said, "Don't hesitate." So, I bought the property, along with the challenges it presented and the promises still waiting to be fulfilled.

I knew that I would pull back the ugly floral drapes, which had kept the healing sun from entering the lonely cottage. I understood how laughter, entwined lovers, celebrations, and music would create a new harmony for the house, and for all who would became a part of it. My heart embraced the challenge to infuse this forlorn space with the joys of living.

Two summers passed without a return visit from my fisherman. I looked for his angular face with the unflinching eyes, but he didn't come back to his old spot. Maybe he didn't like the sounds of children playing or a bunch of city

Helen Gioulis
Philadelphia, PA

folks laughing and having drinks on the new deck. Probably, the old, quiet days were more to his liking. Still, I hoped that he would remember his special corner.

Time by the pond has its own cadence and seductive flow. Everyone who spent time at the house succumbed to pond staring. It was one of the joys of waterside living, and sometimes the highlight of the day. The cushioned chairs on the back deck were the orchestra seats to an ever-changing performance on a perfectly lit stage. The morning light gave depth and reflection to the water especially on crisp fall mornings. When the pond mirrored the autumn hues of the shoreline, it looked like you could walk on a path of golden leaves and dive into the shore's crimson depths. In the afternoon the light tap danced on the water's surface kicking up sparkles. And as the setting sun's rays painted the sky in rich magentas, the water, not to be upstaged, reflected the same magnificent tones.

Dock sitting, second only to pond staring, took place on the rickety wooden dock that swayed gently whenever a boat passed by. The wake created a comforting motion as gentle as the sway of a hammock. I shared the dock with the duck family that liked to leave behind a few feathers as a note of thanks. This year the family consisted of five little ones, who fell into formation with Mom at the front and Dad bringing up the rear. She ran a tight ship, and every day just before sunset, she steered them to the safe marsh area for the night.

In the warm late-day rays the dragonflies draped in their translucent greens, blues and purples dipped, swerved and mated in mid-air. These lithe dancers skimmed the water, and thrilled their audience with their grace and lightness. I applauded this grand performance and said, "Bravo, beautiful ones." And for an encore, the damsel flies folded their wings and rested peacefully on my arm, while the larger dragonflies relaxed with outstretched wings by my feet. That's dock sitting at its best.

Helen Gioulis
Philadelphia, PA

One sunny afternoon as I turned to watch a red dragonfly land on the yellow bloom of a water lily, I spotted my fisherman perched on a jutting rock about fifty yards away. I sat stone still savoring his return and enjoying the moment. He wasn't fishing, just taking in the scene and contemplating his universe. He was a striking figure in his blue-gray garb and taller than I had remembered. Unlike our first encounter, he didn't take off. Instead, the great blue heron turned his head and looked directly at me. He gave me a long cool stare, and then with a studied nonchalance turned his gaze away.

We shared a perfect August day—he perched on his rock, me on my dock. Two kindred souls bound by the peace and beauty of the pond.

***

Zibette Dean
Edgecomb, ME

Truck

Ford 150
spit-and-polish
shiny black

MAINE   Jul. 14
2014XM
VETERAN

VIETNAM XOOO
PRISONERS XOOO

at passenger window
small hand with sparkly polish

Sally Belenardo
Branford, CT

The Kite Flier

To kill some time, he flew
a kite so far and high
a gust of wild wind blew
it down across the sky,

ending the wayward flight
atop a dogwood tree.
It fluttered at a height
where he could get it free,

and not defile the view.
Instead, he left the park,
with better things to do
before the day grew dark.

Days after, in the sun,
those walking past would meet
a robin who'd begun
her nest nearby, her feet

entangled in the string,
and, at her side, the shred
of hay she failed to bring,
her lifeless wings outspread.

Kate Leigh
Portsmouth, NH

Apples: from Sabbath Day Lake Shaker Village

Apple trees, winterberry,
Milkweeds in the pines,
Fallen fence encased in
Grape thicket's vines.
Many hands to work here,
Many hearts to God.
By miles of battered wire wall,
By mounds of garden clod.
Pick an apple off the ground,
Or brussels sprout, froze hard,
Someone planted lavender,
Someone picked red chard.

***

Dark Is Pale

Dark is pale, light intense
The tuxedo cat slips
Beneath the back fence
At day break, delaying
The ivy-nest birds from
Seed congregating.
Still hangs the silver moon
Like a maid's silky slip
Or a shiny teaspoon
Soon-sinking mystery
Momentary cat gone
Birds back in the tree

Bill Eberle
Thomaston, ME

Climbing Time

In succeeding years
our wisdom is seen
                    for what it is

invention and tender folly

as we go forward
imagining mountains
rising ever higher
to see what we thought we knew
on the trails below

illuminated
simplified
and disproved

sweet memories
misted ridges

and blankets of leaves

Before us more mist
assumed
            or gifted
                        revelations

more follies
to be seen
at a later time
as simple good hearted
wishes

Bill Eberle
Thomaston, ME

flurries
     favors
          fevers

and fortune

Remember the boy
who swam in the air

immersed his whole being
in feeling and absorbing
     without knowing

Old man dreaming
catching wisps
         of what is
     and was

evaporating now
    as words
        on paper

Peggy Trojan
Brule, WI

Baseball Mom

for Laura

I came to your games,
Little League to high school varsity.
Froze wearing sleeping bags,
shivered in pouring rain.
Sat on steel bleachers in blazing sun
through extra innings, thinking
I should be making supper.
Drove to out of town games,
kept my tongue
when rude fans yelled advice,
screaming just how
you could have made that run.
Knew all the players,
my screechy cheering ready,
my hands clapped red
for winning hits.
One would assume
I am a serious baseball fan.
I did not spend all those
afternoons for baseball.
I came to watch you.

Patricia T. Graves
York, ME

Korean Eyes

It was the tenth day of unyielding gray. Maneuvering around the leftovers of record-setting winds—brittle branches, washed-up rocks, slick seaweed—we were picking our way along the cliff walk when without prelude the clouds shifted unveiling brilliant, lavish light. The sun on high beams. As if echoing a call, a corresponding spaciousness of spirit radiated through me—floating me back to 1976. I turned to Larry, my husband, my life companion, "I didn't realize how much I was missing the sun until it showed up. This feels like the first day Joy smiled at us."

It was a Wednesday. Joy Elisabeth, soft in yellow terry, was enthroned in the maple high chair. From behind her wisps of black hair peaked the puppy dog decal I'd applied after sanding off the remnants of a duck worn thin by the noggins of the previous generation—Larry, Barb, Nan and Sue. One of Larry's leather belts linked baby to chair. Since thirty-year-old high chairs did not come equipped with seat belts, we had been compelled to improvise after Joy had disappeared beneath the tray the first time her cotton-clad bottom met the newly varnished seat.

Although she was old enough to sit in a high chair, we were brand new parents. Only five days before we had driven to John F. Kennedy Airport to greet our six-month-old daughter who had arrived subdued and dazed by the seventeen-hour journey from Seoul. The car ride from New York City to our home in Massachusetts was uneventful. In 1976 there were no airbags so Joy's carseat was perched between us. She was remarkably compliant when we buckled her in—her only gesture to latch onto the cloth diaper that I had taken out to catch stray droplets of milk. Immediately our daughter (a word that raised goose bumps on my flesh) brought the cloth to her face and slipped two fingers into her

Patricia T. Graves
York, ME

mouth. The diaper's whiteness reflected the lights of passing cars. Joy was mesmerized—neither asleep nor awake.

The other houses on our street were dark when we pulled into our driveway. I carried our little one past the welcome sign created by neighbors—taking note of the blueberry muffins on the counter and the stuffed bunny propped beside them. We climbed the stairs to introduce Joy to her room—the floral paper, fluffy throw rugs, newly painted furniture and Priscilla curtains. At the airport the escort had changed Joy's diaper before presenting her to us; now it was my turn. No sooner had I placed her on her back than she was showing off her roll-over prowess—her reflexes much quicker than mine so that every time I'd roll her onto her back she'd flip onto her stomach. Making the first decision of many to submit to my child's will, I did my best to secure the diaper pins while she lay face-down.

Despite their sporting six-to-nine month labels, the first several PJ's pulled from neat piles in her dresser overflowed Joy's limbs by inches. As one discarded outfit after another lay scattered on the floor and furniture, I settled on a hand-me-down three-to-six-month sleeper donated by friends who had twice welcomed daughters from Korea. Our little one was finally ready to be tucked in.

We'd gone modern and white when choosing a crib—bedecking it with the bluebirds and rainbow quilt hand-sewn by Grandma and a miniature Snoopy sitting in non-dog-like fashion on his rump, legs extended straight out. We planted kisses on the flat spot between Korean eyes and lay Joy on her tummy—comfort diaper clutched close, mobile playing "Brahms' Lullaby," night light on, table lamp off, door ajar, queen bed enticing weary parents. But before we could pull up the covers and sink into sleep, a full-throttle howl erupted from across the hall. A night of pacing, rocking, feeding, burping, toy-offering, and diaper-checking ensued until at last, as the first glimmers of November dawn peered through gauzy curtains, Joy collapsed on her new dad's shoulder.

Patricia T. Graves
York, ME

A few short hours later we trundled our daughter off to see Dr. Leader. Our friends with Korean-born children said he knew what to check for. "See those splotches," the pediatrician pointed to Joy's bottom, "she's had a rash recently—perhaps from a bug that gave her diarrhea." As though to confirm the doctor's supposition, a day later Larry and I became frequent fliers in our bathroom. In the midst of juggling trips to the toilet, throw-up basins, diaper changes and feedings, the phone rang. The call was from a couple we'd met at the airport. Their daughter, Melissa, had arrived on the same plane as Joy. They wondered how we were doing and mentioned that they'd all been sick. Blessedly, Grandma came to spell us for a day—not letting us know until weeks later that the bug that had traveled halfway across the world had found her intestines, too.

Nearly a week after Joy's arrival—our digestive tracts finally re-regulated—we prepared to sit around the dining room table with our little girl. Meals were a time when you could count on having Joy's attention. The doctor said she would stop eating when she'd had enough so to feed her as much as she wanted. We never discovered her shut-off valve; however, and finally settled on five jars of baby food a day plus cereal and milk as the limit. Joy ingested her food with great concentration, pushing it in with two fingers then opening up for the next mouthful. Her intense gaze was on the food, not on the parent feeding her, and although she was clearly receiving what she most desired her face revealed no visible expression of pleasure.

In fact when we greeted Joy with delight, hugged and kissed her or offered up songs and toys, we were consistently met with impassivity. After a few days, I believe I nearly forgot that babies of this age were capable of smiling. Now as I think back on that time, I realize that Joy was in all likelihood depressed.

Even though we had read the materials recommended by the adoption agency, we were not fully prepared for the

Patricia T. Graves
York, ME

effects that great change imposes on a six-month-old's psyche. Yoo Jin Mee, now known as Joy Elisabeth Graves, had been abruptly plunked into a culture where people had big round eyes and pale skin. Broad vowel sounds poured from our mouths—strange, perhaps even frightening in their foreignness. Instead of the fermented spiciness of kimchi wafting through the air, our kitchen aromas featured coffee, spaghetti sauce and apple crisp. On top of all that, she was expected to sleep in a crib instead of a mat on the floor and to sit in a bouncy seat as opposed to being carried on her caregiver's back. From what we could glean from the records, we were her fourth home in six months. It would have been difficult under these circumstances for her to experience a sense of certainty as to who her people were no matter who was caring for her; but certainly the two Americans of Irish/English descent who were now hovering over her didn't come close to meeting whatever expectations a Korean-born six-month-old might have about her caregivers. Although to us, Joy was a dream-come-true; to her we were, in all probability, more like "the bumps in the night."

So on that first day of December 1976, we were doing what we knew to do to nurture our daughter. She had just devoured applesauce and green beans and after a brief protest, had complied with face and finger washing. Larry scooted her chair up close to the table, and I sprinkled a few Cheerios onto the tray to divert her from ogling our meatloaf and mashed potatoes. We reached out to hold her hands in preparation to say our family's grace and then it happened— Joy's stoic Asian stare transformed itself into a great big cloud-clearing grin. It took a moment to register, to soak in the warmth that was washing over us—our child was smiling, our child's deep dark almond eyes were lit up, our child's eyes were meeting our eyes. The meatloaf turned cold, the potato congealed but the pictures taken that evening attest to the sustenance contained in one baby's smile.

Of course, we had not seen the end of being rendered

Patricia T. Graves
York, ME

powerless by our daughter's impenetrable stare and the challenges of many more adjustments lay ahead, but we had had an experience of connection—an experience to give us hope that some day we would, indeed, truly be her people.

***

Andrew Badger
Douglasville, GA

Last Leaf Turned

No leaves remain
in this old book.
Pages once penned
by schoolboy hand
slowly becomes
crimped, terse,
ambiguous,
as I write
inexorably
down the inside
back cover.

I await the day
I'm abruptly
translated
into a divine
edition scribed
and signed
by God himself
who shuts and
shelves the book
next to those
who await me.

Corinne Davis
Montpelier, VT

Snowflake Bentley

Bentley left from his walk here on earth July twelfth, twenty
    eleven
The Lord called out to him in an instant as he needed him in
    heaven

We do not get to choose when we will be called home
It leaves those left behind hurting, empty and alone

We all must trust that Bentley's life is fully in God's hands
And that when he was called home, it was for a reason,
That he fits into a much greater plan,

Knowing this does not seem to lessen the grieving family's
    pain
In fact, at times, they may even feel that they are going
    insane

Bentley, we celebrated you coming into this world,
and we celebrate you as you depart;

Your memory will live on in all of us, tucked away preciously
in our hearts

We will fondly remember you and our hearts will ache for you
    too,

We will remember your touch and your warm, soft embrace.
And that turned up smile on one side of your face,

That little twinkle that you had in your eye; sometimes
    saying
I'm a little bit shy,

Corinne Davis
Montpelier, VT

Mom and Dad will remember you calling out to them,
Wishing they could hear your voice over and over again,

Sweetie Grammy and Grampa Stanley are keeping you safe,
With Mittens happily in your lap, in a heavenly place

We all love you so much, Bentley

***

Mr. Squirrel

Mr. Squirrel beckoning to me,
Swinging through the trees like a chimpanzee
He sways and reaches and jumps around
Toying with my attention like a mime or clown
So furry and fat as he sits huddled on the fence,
Dutifully ready to avail his defense
Incessantly he cracks open each peanut or seed
While enemies embark out of their own greed
It is odd how his eyes are on each side of his head
Rather than like us, we look straight instead
He doesn't have a care and is back each day
He softens me like a child in mindless play

Elmae Passineau
Wausau, WI

Little Woman

Pale brown hair brushes her chin,
head bent deep in concentration,
Lily takes in the lives
of Jo and Meg and Beth and Amy
Just seven years old
she reads the child's version,
legs tucked under her
on the soft old couch
oblivious to her surroundings
She sits in a circle of golden lamplight
while snow falls silently outside the windows
and the scent of simmering stew
hints of supper and a comfortable evening

And suddenly, *Grandma, Grandma!*
Guess what happened!
All giggles and surprise and wonder
What, what?
More giggles and shyness now,
I can't tell you!
Blue eyes animated with delight,
a brush with novelty—
Here, you read it!
I read.
Mr. Brooke has kissed Meg.

Robert B. Moreland
Pleasant Prairie, WI

Bella Detesta Matribus[1]

Fourth of July, flags, parades; banners fly
all the while six thousand moms wonder why
the fine young men and women that they raised
were sent away to distant sands to die.

Red, white and blue patriotism praised
sacrifices recount, barbecue braised.
Somewhere lost in her bedroom are the sobs
as she hears the president's words amazed.

Her best were sent there to their G.I. jobs,
she weeps, the hope of her grandchildren robbed.
Composed, joins the celebration at last
ignoring the pain, sees the faceless mob.

How many more go, what now comes to pass?
We bury our future, look to the past.
Six thousand moms heave a collective sigh,
Old Glory draped caskets and flags half mast.

[1]"War, the horror of mothers" Horace

Marjorie Bixler
Fort Worth, TX

A Picasso Morning

The alarm jangles,
jerks me from sleep.
I face the looking glass.
One eye swims across the bridge
to its twin on the other side.
Stiff joints twang like the guitar
the gaunt man played.

Today I'll salvage past mistakes,
a touch-up here, a brush stroke there,
another blue day, framed.

***

Amy Lavin Liston
Portland, ME

Finally

Snow expires
        in a ministry of light,

  sings its own elegy
            sotto voce on the rooftops,

soothes raw trees
            in the attitude of angels;

spare sigh between the falling
            and the failing.

Bill Tucker
Aurora, OH

A Very Short Story about Old Friends

The Tulane Odd Couple—Howell and Bill—Felix and Oscar—fastidious and earthy. Over sixty years of association—about a half dozen of those years as somewhat reluctant teacher and somewhat reluctant student and fifty-five years as close (and tolerant) friends.

When I returned to Tulane to do graduate work and become an instructor on the Engineering faculty, it was reported some months after the fact by some mutual friend (probably Charlie Roland) that Howell had asked the rhetorical question "How can God (or maybe Lee Johnson) be so unkind that he puts Tucker in the office next to me?" It was several years later that he revised his evaluation of God's kindness when he discovered the boundless physical charms of Bridget Bardot in the aptly titled movie "And God Created Woman."

And Chloe, the elegant woman Howell had the good fortune to marry at the beginning of my senior year, matched Bridget in every perfection of form. If Chloe spoke French, I was unaware of it. But that was a blessing, because I didn't have to read the subtitles before I would make my always clever ripostes.

And it came to pass that Howell and Chloe moved from their cliff dwelling (an apartment in a bleak building on St. Charles Avenue, if I recall accurately) and joined Betty Lee (a woman equal in elegance and physical charm to Chloe and Bridget and married to Mr. Wonderful—that's me) and me in the more congenial atmosphere (and the company of the poor and near poor) on Lauricella Avenue in Azalea Gardens.

Here, it seems that some of the rough edges that had so disconcerted Howell in the past were worn from me by the passing of time, the necessary community of living close together, Betty Lee and Chloe pretty much ignoring any peev-

Bill Tucker
Aurora, OH

ishness either one of us might have, the fact the Tucker's
Kathleen and the Peebles' Howie did the same bad things in
their diapers, and the sharing of a power lawnmower that
was ancient when one of us bought it. (I don't remember
who.)

I believe the incident that proved Howell had accepted me
as an unavoidable social burden was his allowing me to open
the door of his 1957 Cadillac Coupe DeVille without wearing
gloves. This also seemed to mark the time when he intro-
duced me to his good friend, Charlie Roland of the Tulane
History faculty. Through these early years and all the years
since, Charlie, who has a little of both Felix and Oscar in
him, has become the perfect insulator between two disparate
personalities. Charlie's elegant wife, Allie Lee, would also
come to join Betty Lee and Chloe as they watched in mild
amusement the interaction of the trio that could now be better identified as Larry, Curly and Moe.

***

Thomas Peter Bennett
Bradenton, FL

Beach Refugees

Each high-tide wave brings
immigrant shells—
    augers, miters, and mussels
    to the white sand beach.
Their boats of passage are
    pen shells, seaweed,
    driftwood, and sponges.

Sylvia Little-Sweat
Wingate, NC

Sleeves

The November day
Mother died, I sat
alone beside her bed,
laid my palm on her
arm, the back of my
hand against her still,
warm side before
its heat could flee.
How long would
a faint heart beat
before it cracked,
splintered memory?

When my sister and I
stripped the room of
Mother's final years,
we sorted books,
throws, and clothes
for those by time still
confined to assisted
care. But I reclaimed
her purple coat to wear
each dawn of grief—
its sleeves of fleece
to hug the child in me.

Patrick T. Randolph
Kalamazoo, MI

Wisconsin Winter Woods

Cut down an old tree,
Chop up the wood,
Split the wood,
Haul the wood,
Burn the wood.

Listen—
           a forest of stories,
                 flickering in the stove.

***

7th Grade Crush: Modern Orpheus

He'd look at her eyes:
Undulating waves of sea,
Blue ripples in blue;

She never saw his shy glance—
He never saw her—look back.

***

Minnesota Lighthouse Man

Old laughter
           fills his eyes—
                echoes with light.

Maxine B. Weintraub
Wayland, MA

Country Fair

What a lucky girl to have an entire day at the fair. Cows and pigs and goats and horses and fried dough and deep fried onion rings and cotton candy and taffy apples and hot dogs with sauerkraut. Balloons. Donkey rides and a haunted house. Horse pulling contests and bearded ladies. Pie baking competitions and hand sewn aprons and baseball pitching. And here I am now, a bit worn out, swinging in my chair, stopped at the top of the Ferris wheel, looking out at the fairgrounds as the lights go out one by one. I have tried every ride but the roller coaster and now that I sit up here and hear the last shouts and screams from those brave riders I wonder why I was always too afraid to try that.

It was a glorious day. The sun shone down on us all and the sky was blue. Truth is, there were two spectacular short thunderstorms. Winds gusting, and trash flying and little children crying and people scurrying for cover. But the storms passed and the sun came out.

I pretty much behaved myself. I gave a crying child the doll I had won at the penny pitch and was tempted to keep a silk scarf I found on the path near the ladies' room. I returned it to the Lost and Found.

I loved the games but never won much. That doll at the penny pitch. The darts were hard. Duck shooting was ridiculous. I ate a lot of sweet stuff and salty stuff and spent all of my money and as dusk came I noticed that most of my friends had left. A few had left much earlier in the day. Thunderstorms, I supposed. And now I am here as twilight fades and the end of the day and the end of the fair are coming on fast. Sitting up here on top of the Ferris wheel.

Soon I will be deposited on the ground, walk happily but wearily to my car and head home. How lucky to have had such a glorious day at the fair. The truth is, even though my

Maxine B. Weintraub
Wayland, MA

friends have left, I am not ready to leave. I want to stay here
with the smells and the tastes and the sights and the noise
and the music.

***

Sylvia Little-Sweat
Wingate, NC

Closure

*Miss Juel is strolling across the streets of gold
and she don't need no J. C. Penny's shoes,*
consoled Steve the mortician who had known
Mother for years, had buried other family before.

She always looked so pretty and smelled so good,
he eulogized while we planned Mother's final
rites. When asked whether we had certain clothes
to bury Mother in, my sister replied, *Maybe a pretty*

shroud. At once Steve countered, *But they don't
look like Miss Juel—they look like something
an old woman would wear.* At ninety-one Mother
was already ageless in Steve's eyes, and he would

see that she held that place. So we chose from
her clothes a new navy suit and bright red blouse.
To him Mother was an orchid on a slender stem who
even in Death's repose rivaled the lily and the rose.

Earl Weigelt
Winslow, ME

The Gritty Annoyances

So, riddle me this...

I think I get the Big Ones,
the loss and pain and grief.
It's the little things that strike me dumb,
that leave me asking, "Why?"

It's the mechanical break;
the forgotten thing;
the nagging hip and throbbing back;
that nasty black ice patch;

The thigh-deep slush on Eagle Lake;
the white caps on Caucomgomoc;
The rod tip in the tailgate;
and the auger that won't start!

The license on the bedroom floor—
the warden at my pickup door;
the hole in the net; my missing vest,
and my maps left in the drawer!

I wonder if it's conspiracy,
or if all the blame belongs to me.
But no matter what, I won't quit!
I must get outside... and I will!

And perhaps in His mercy
when the Almighty takes me,
He'll let me in on the joke.

Belva Ann Prycel
Alna, ME

A Marsh Memory

I spend my days on rock-clad peaks,
Under the shade of pine and spruce;
But within my soul is a voice that speaks
Of a wanderer's uneasy truce.
I see the light of the northern coast,
Sharp-edged, like steel, uncompromised;
By haze or heat or mists to float
And filter colour through my eyes.

The river smoke soon disappears,
Into a blue unsullied sky;
That changes slow as evening nears
To thin dark streaks that fade and die.
No birdsong music fills the air,
No softening shadows on the sea,
No mystery near horizons where
Some muted light hangs lingeringly.

Just edge and detail, sharpened line,
Some depths of blues that overlay
The rocks that border shoals, define
Their lithic silhouettes of gray.

But marsh remembered! Grasses green
And fill the shallows as they bear
The silty sands that mark the sheen
Of morning tidelines' passage there.
A feathery brush of foxtail sheaf,
A breath of bay winds, whispering, sends,
A breeze caressing blade and leaf,
In curling grasses on the winds.

(continued)

Belva Ann Prycel
Alna, ME

In muddy banks I see the Light
Reflected, changing, ever soft;
Above my head, I hear the flight
Of birds that hover high, aloft.

The marsh is a diffused Monet,
But northern shores are granite hard;
The sky above and earth both lay
Within a palette, sharp, like sard.
My old allegiance will not die
The deepest longings bide and stay
For mist-glazed shorelines and the sky
The salty marshes by the bay.

***

Into the Night

Carry me into the night, like a child,
Where the June eve speaks and the firefly glows,
Where the air holds the scent of an island rose.

Into the night, on an evening mild,
When the wind walks softly down pebbled lanes,
And the last light of day discreetly wanes.

Carry me into the night, I'll speak
To the mourning dove and the owls around
In music, far past voice or sound.

Into the night, and there I'll dream
All I have loved, all I have known,
Beneath a sleeping moon,
alone.

Beth Marshall Jack
Lake Forest, CA

Stasis

I felt silence plait and stitch
careful patterns across the tablecloth,
our floral design in the vase, slumped over
like a faded daguerreotype, now a blank stasis;
reminds me of a page
you read earlier, how our daughter earned high marks
in algebra, could solve equations,
knew formulas by punch of a button,
blithely translates foil method into solutions,
fills vacancies with a stubby pencil,
bringing order to the puzzle.

Our eyes meet, across the expanse of china and glass,
questions lined up with silver forks and knives and spoons,
all polished with a cloth, until they gleamed
like surgical instruments,
before anesthesia probes—amputates spaces
no longer viable. I could feel my focus
narrowing—shrink, then pull toward
your wan face behind a bowl of olives
diluted in brine, how your cloth napkin
blots up the excess.

How do we decode and elucidate the theorem
of a sigh, a heartbeat, a kiss?
You snuffed the candles out
before I could touch your wrist.

Nancy Holmes
Newcastle, ME

Mowing the Lower Field

It was the first time her father let her mow hay. Ever since she was six or seven, whenever she could get away from her mother, she had trotted after the mower, carrying a pitchfork to clear the cutter bar when it got clogged with grass. Her father never smiled, but she could read the pride and pleasure on his face when she trotted up and whisked away the jammed grass in front of the mower, so he didn't have to climb down from the tractor. Now her legs were long enough to reach the clutch and brakes. Ever since she was heavy enough to push down the pedals, she had been driving it standing up, balancing herself by hanging onto the steering wheel. She had no doubt in her ability. But her mother was furious. Her mother wanted her in the kitchen with an apron over her rounding hips.

Her father never voiced it, but she could see pride in his eyes as he sternly instructed her. "Keep your mind on the job, Amy. You've got to listen to the equipment. This tractor is old! If anything sounds different, you shut her right off and come get me. Got it?" He slapped the grey hood over the idling engine. "And listen to that sicklebar. You gotta keep the PTO speed up. If it starts to sound kind of heavy and labored, it's getting clogged with grass and you're probably not revving her up enough. You've got the pitchfork aboard, so if you can't clear it by backing up, you'll have to get down and clear it. And don't, whatever you do, get your hands around that sicklebar! Even when it's stopped, there may still be enough tension in the Pitman rod to ..." He held up a hand with four and a half fingers. She listened politely, but she knew the whole thing. Had known it for years.

She wheeled into the field, engaged the PTO, revved up the engine and dropped the sicklebar. She knew every tick and chug of the old engine, and every nuance of clatter as the

Nancy Holmes
Newcastle, ME

long knife with its row of sharp triangular sections slid blur-ry-fast back and forth in the slotted steel bar. The grass flowed over the cutter and dropped to the ground in a neat shining sheet. She was full of power. Competent. When she came to the corner of the field down by the alders, she lifted the bar, stopped and backed up to make the 90 degree turn. She started forward and dropped the bar as she had watched her father do a thousand times. It dropped too late, leaving a line of uncut grass. Not as easy as it looked. She raised the bar, backed up and tried again. When she came to the down grass she had cut on the first try, the fingers of the sicklebar picked up the loose grass and in an instant the sharp sections were jammed with wads of grass. She tried backing up to wipe the grass off on the ground, but it was a hopeless mess. Shutting off the PTO to stop the snicking knife, she climbed down and cleared the grass with the pitch-fork. She took a quick glance toward the house. Hoped her parents weren't looking.

Every corner was easier. The third time she went around the alder corner her timing was perfect. She told herself to quit thinking how good she was and concentrate on listening and watching and paying attention. The lush grass along the alder edge fell smoothly behind. Over the noise of the engine and the clatter of the mower, she heard a soft, brief squeal. A belt slipping? At that moment a doe jumped out of the alders right in front of the tractor. Amy stopped in amaze-ment, watching the doe. It ran two jumps into the field, turned abruptly and bounced back into the alders. Silly deer. Wasn't the tractor making enough noise to keep her hidden? Amy peered into the brush trying to see the deer, but it was gone. She raised the cutter bar a few inches so it wouldn't catch the down grass and clog again. When she looked back to finesse the timing of dropping the bar, she saw a fawn struggling in the mowed grass. Amy turned away, covering her face with her hands. Her foot came off the clutch and the tractor bucked and stalled. Well, that was a dumb girl thing to do. She'd seen calves die; she'd killed chickens. She was tough. She jumped off the tractor and ran back, holding her breath. Maybe she could take it home and nurse it back to health. But the fawn was too badly cut to live. She would have to put it out of its misery. She looked up at the farmhouse. No one in sight. This was hers to take care of. Standing over the fawn, she fought back tears. Sissy! She took a deep breath, went to the tractor tool box, and managed with shaking hands to open the box and get out the big hammer.

After she had done what must be done, she went back to the tractor feeling sick and weak. Then she remembered that fawns usually come in pairs, and dread of repeating the carnage stopped her in her tracks. She would have to look for the twin. She started a methodical search, walking back and forth, back and forth under the hard June sun. She pictured the doe peeking through the alders, watching her try to hunt down the remaining baby. She spoke to the doe. "It's okay, Mama. I'm trying to find it for you." As she turned at the end of a pass, she saw the neighbor boy striding down the field. Bobby was shirtless, tan and lean, but his shoulders were starting to broaden. Moose legs walked below tattered cut-off jeans. She stopped and waited for him, hoping, just hoping, that he could help somehow without making her feel like a dumb girl.

"Hi, Amy," he said. "I saw you walking. Did you hit a fawn?"

She nodded, trying hard to look calmly concerned. Boys don't cry, and she was as good as any boy. "Yuh. I'm looking to see if there's a twin."

His voice skipped between boy and man. "I figured." He walked parallel to her a few feet away, searching in the tall grass. They walked in silence back and forth for twenty minutes. Finally he stopped beside her, shaking his head. "Seems as if we'd have found it if there was one. We can't hunt all day." He looked away from her awkwardly. "The

Nancy Holmes
Newcastle, ME

other one must be dead?"

She turned away, too. She couldn't count on her face to stay stoic. "Yeah. I had to kill it."

"Uh!" he grunted. They walked back to the mower and looked down at the little gold body, so elegantly spotted with white.

He squatted down and gently gathered it in his arms, stood up and pushed through the alders to lay it down carefully in a shady patch of ferns. She stood beside him; saw the blood on his arms. "I have water on the tractor." They made their way back onto the sunny field. She took a filthy rag out of the tool box and, making a face, poured water on it. He held his arms out in such a vulnerable way, but they were not the thin arms of a boy. She stroked the dripping rag over arms rounded and corded with muscle. She glanced shyly at his face and thought she saw the hint of tears in the corners of his eyes. Boys do cry? They had known each other since they were babies, and even then he didn't cry much. She felt tears start in her own eyes. They forced a quick smile at each other.

"Thanks, Bobby!"

"Sure, Amy. Tough luck."

He turned and started up the hill, his hands in his pockets; she went back to the tractor.

Rozell Caldwell
Jackson, TN

MisEducation

I float
As if on waves
Up and down
The 8th grade hallway
From one reading class
to another
Discovering
A majority of 8th graders
unable to read

The books
On the shelf
Are whispering
But no one's listening
As we come
To the end of the day
The knowledge we seek
Is huddled in dark unopened books
That remain on the shelf

***

Patrick T. Randolph
Kalamazoo, MI

Halloween in Turkish Village

Old storyteller:
Statue in the public square—
Listens to the Night.

Diane Colvin Reitz
Winter Park, FL

Homeless Boy

When I drove by,
you were animated, waving
your arms, talking
to yourself and I thought,
"What a crazy teenager."

You walked up to the
Metro bus on the corner but
you did not get on.
You continued to talk, pace
back and forth like one
trying to explain to God....

You looked at me like an injured,
impaled animal, while my sports car was running,
my job waiting and my nice life humming.

I stared into your face.

It is your face that I cannot forget...
the still and queer horror.

Sunken eyes, black circles,
as if you had been hit hard
between your wanting eyes.

His body, thin, lank and wandering.
The boy in deep dark trouble—frightening.

Diane Colvin Reitz
Winter Park, FL

But, I kept on driving down the
road slowly—stretching to look in the
rear view mirror, the boy getting
smaller eventually gone from view.

So many others had driven by,
wondering what the hell was
wrong with that boy?

Wrong question. We should
have been asking
what is wrong with us?

***

Kate Leigh
Portsmouth, NH

Fish Story

You flopped into my life like a fish on a deck,
Your scales sang with the scent of the sea
Yet also with wool, and snow and wood smoke,
Such combination well suited for me.
But then came in the lure of the fin
And you slipped overboard to the ocean again.

P. C. Moorehead
North Lake, WI

A Piece of Wood

I drift,
far from shore,
a piece of wood,
without a home.

No deep rich earth
to nourish me,
no glade to gladden me.
I am alone.

I drift.
The water soothes me.
The sun gladdens me.
I learn new ways.

I am nourished.

                              ***

Sunning

The several summers of sun—
I am in one.
I feel good—glad, not sad.
How nice to be
summered in sun.

Craig Merrow
Sanford, ME

The Stork

Once upon a time, there was a stork who was born into a middle class family. He had a happy childhood and did well in school, made the football team, and graduated with honors. Then he got drafted into the Army Air Force and served his country well during World War II. After the war, he went to college under the GI Bill and earned a degree in Business Administration.

Putting his education to work, he identified a niche market and started a baby delivery service. The stork soon found that he had a pretty good racket going for a high-demand product; business was brisk, with the orders just pouring in. It wasn't long before he built up The Stork Company into a successful enterprise, launched an IPO, and had shares being traded on Wall Street. His stocks soared in value, as he had the entire market to himself, and people were eager to invest in his company, product, and services.

It was easy to place an order; all you had to do was look in the back pages of *The Saturday Evening Post* for The Stork Company ad and send for the catalog. When you received it, you filled out the order form, checked off the options you wanted, included a check or money order, and mailed it in. Sometimes he even offered a two-for-one special. Then you waited about nine months, because each baby was made to order, and they had a huge backlog, but he always came through, delivering a bundle of joy to your doorstep.

With a solid business plan, low overhead and high profit margins, everything was just fine and dandy at The Stork Company. Until one day, sometime in the Sixties...

...Somebody invented sex.

It didn't take long for people to figure out that they didn't need to order a baby from the stork when you could just build one yourself from scratch. It still took nine months, of

Craig Merrow
Sanford, ME

course, but it was a lot cheaper and you didn't need to fill out an order form, or even buy the kit. As the do-it-yourself approach gained momentum, the stork saw his market share shrink and the company stock plummeted. By the time 1970 rolled around, he found he could no longer compete and liquidated his remaining inventory before he closed his doors for good. He was disappointed about it, as he had built his fame and fortune around the baby delivery business. Down, but not out, he still had good entrepreneurial skills and a keen eye for opportunities; drawing on his vast experience, he set out to reinvent himself and established a whole new enterprise to meet the demand of expecting mothers.

And that, in a nutshell, is how the stork got into the business of selling Vlasic Pickles.

***

Mark D. Biehl
Hales Corners, WI

Costume Change

Finches fluffed
To twice their
Summer sleek.
Ochre, olive drab
All look alike
Until
The solstice
Signals.

Robert Witte
Waldoboro, ME

Ides of March

Crumpled quilting of old snow
patched upon
Rumpled fabric of dead brown grass.
Broad ribbon of gravel road, broidered
with tread-track stitches,
And hemmed with black, hungry ditches
That ate cars and trucks when blizzards
First laid snow-quilt upon the ground.

Now, "Eichen stehen kalt und krumm,[1]"
And green-black fir and pine are all around.
It is our joy, though; we know the signs of old.
This dreary cover-cloth's the setting
Whereon the summer's gold
And green of crops, grass, weeds, fruit will grow.

So welcome "mud season," or call it spring;
It enters in the joy of our hearts (perhaps Ostara),
The year come 'round again.

[1]A line from "Peat Bog Soldiers," a song written by
Jewish prisoner, Die Moorsoldaten, in a Nazi concentration camp.

T. Blen Parker
Richmond, ME

Little Red Brick Schoolhouse

Pownalborough School ~ 1961

Closing my eyes, my mind's-eye sees
wooden floors, freshly oiled
where thundering feet tread,
desktops sanded down,
varnished now, shiny and new,
featured thoughtfully-carved initials last semester.

Unassuming pupils with open minds,
anticipate the unknown, as they
stare in wonder at inkwells from decades passed.
Only empty holes in wooden desktops,
these circles, if they could talk,
might reveal deep, dark secrets,
remnants of history....

Rows of seats rest on ornate hinges of
wrought iron, freshly painted shiny black,
now folded down from the front
of each desk waiting to be adopted
by a new pupil, in a new grade, for a new year.
One room, once again filled
with chatter and chaotic action.
Anxious students, collectively
sharing accounts
of summer adventures, first loves,
amazing discoveries.
Family stories whirl around
in the early fall air, like mini tornadoes.

T. Blen Parker
Richmond, ME

Sporting a new coat of blacking,
a small, boxy woodstove
stands before each student
cloaked in their freshly-pressed school clothes.
A gleaming silver stovepipe,
wrapped in chicken wire
prevented children from being burned,
provided a drying rack
for hanging winter's wet mittens and hats.

One dedicated to each grade,
double blackboards were posted
at the head wall of the classroom,
awaiting the day's lessons.
Teacher, Mrs. Doris Souviney, wrote
homework instructions imparting
her wisdom, scripted in new chalk.

An already old oak roll top desk,
with its top rolled back,
presented "teacher necessities."
Peeking from within mysterious
cubbies and drawers lived
class roll, extra pencils,
brass lunch bell, office supplies,
test papers and answer sheets.
Thoughtfully prepared items,
collected during summer "break"
by a teacher who genuinely cared.

A woodshed chock full of wood,
cut by hand in spring, split, delivered
and stacked on a hot summer day
by a charitable father, big brother or uncle
waited to warm two grades

(continued)

T. Blen Parker
Richmond, ME

of students and one dedicated teacher.
The wood heat comforting,
during a chilly Maine winter
in the little red brick schoolhouse.

Time-out in the woodshed,
furnished an opportunity to reflect
on my schoolroom offense.
Direct eye contact
from Mrs. Souviney's stern face
identified, often precipitated,
a life changing moment,
despite the passive delivery.
No need for raising her voice,
no need for rulers rapping knuckles,
no rush to judgment of the offense,
simple, extremely effective discipline!

A private moment with nature
rather than an assigned chore,
Out in the gravel driveway of the schoolyard,
I stood rewarded,
feeling lucky to be banging
felt erasers free of chalk dust.
A wry smile crossed my face,
when I raised my face upward,
to watch with wonder as
Swango's eagles, soared and circled
through the blue, blue, blueness
of the new autumn sky.

Recess time!
Collectively we breathed in
the crisp fall air of the outdoors in Maine
as we poured single-file

(continued)

T. Blen Parker
Richmond, ME

out the front door.
Classmates chose teams.
Who would be chosen as swing-er?
Who would be the pusher?
Moments of energetic giggles,
pinches and tickles were shared
by those anxious to be the first
on the log pole swing sets,
strung with thick sturdy new rope
and smoothly sanded board seats.
Each swing-er kicked to ride
as high as the clear blue sky
until someone else took their turn.

Black handled brass bell rang out,
time for her class roll call,
Mrs. Souviney checked off each name,
assuring herself everyone was present
before we returned to her classroom.
The long hours pass with lessons
in spelling, reading, arithmetic.
Students always passing notes,
mostly helping out someone else
who doesn't quite "get it" yet.

Finally, lunchtime arrived!
All morning, on a long wooden shelf
at the back of the room near the window,
my square, red-plaid metal lunchbox
joined the row of plain black, silver or Annie Oakley,
Lone Ranger, or Gumby lunchboxes,
crumpled brown paper-bags
wedged in between.

T. Blen Parker
Richmond, ME

As I lift the lid, the aromas filled my nostrils
with various sandwich fillings; bologna,
peanut butter, American cheese with butter or
lunch spread with mayonnaise,
their Wonderbread crusts removed,
all carefully wrapped in waxed paper,
by a mother, aunt or sister's busy hands
earlier that morning.
Forgot your lunch, didn't have
a sandwich? Someone always shared.
We were in this together,
brothers and sisters of both grades, all ages.

A pint of white milk
in a waxy cardboard box
sat on ice in an Oakhurst crate,
waiting for each student to enjoy
with their sandwiches.
For others, a drink of cool water,
another choice of beverages
came from the stoneware crock,
spigot drip, drip, dripping
over the oblong black sink,
on the sideboard in the back
corner of the classroom.

No thoughts of botulism, salmonella,
BPU's or melamine hidden
in products imported from China
or other countries where quality of life
was not so important as in the U.S.A.

We felt safe in our *little* red schoolhouse.
We took for granted the significance
of a crisp new American Flag

(continued)

T. Blen Parker
Richmond, ME

hanging above the blackboards
in front of both classes. Students
stood with hands across our hearts
to recite the Pledge of Allegiance each morning.
Fire or civil defense
duck-and-cover drills didn't seem any
more than a chance to escape
from lessons for just a few more moments.
Our innocence prevailed.

My forefinger raised high above my head
signified a request to visit the outhouse,
our restroom, existing in an addition
beyond the classroom.
Permission granted, a nod from the teacher,
I quietly raised from my seat
to venture down the aisle,
under the silver stovepipe wired across the ceiling.
Empty coffee cans hung at leaky intervals,
designed to catch dripping creosote.
Reaching the designated "girls" room door,
I opened the wooden panel door
revealing a short hallway
with yet another door.

Behind the second door
resided a thigh high shelf,
providing two sizes of round holes,
one large and one small.
Strategically placing myself
over the selected cutout,
I reached for a roll of courtesy paper
hanging from the side wall
and, finished my business to
return quickly to afternoon classes.

T. Blen Parker
Richmond, ME

Mrs. Doris Souviney!
A gifted lady with the ability
to settle down 25 or more
unassuming pre-teens
utilizing her secret weapon,
direct eye contact.
Simultaneously helping each student
feel they had the advantage
of a private tutor,
acting as a favorite aunt, she managed
to share a personal moment
with only them.

Whenever one was having a difficult day
or perhaps several in a row,
the courtesy of a discreet private chat
determined whatever the concern.
One always felt the "warm blanket of love"
without so much as a fleeting physical touch.

Her subtle suggestion
insured a pivotal moment
in so many impressionable lives.
Her seemingly psychic abilities
continue to mystify me today!

My eyes are now open,
moist from such vivid memories.
I miss you now as I've missed you
since you departed.

Thank you Mrs. Souviney
for helping us all
prepare for life!!!!!

Ilga Winicov Harrington
Waldoboro, ME

In the Light of One Small Candle

December. Almost time for Christmas, but rain is coming down in sheets. My husband and I are driving home from a concert late at night. The road has become barely visible when we turn into our driveway and the wind, howling though our thick forest of barely visible firs, creates a sense of fear and dread. We finally arrive at the house and see each window decorated with a lighted candle. Suddenly the uncomfortable atmosphere is lifted from the light emanating from each and every candle. After all, we are home. But looking at the light of those candles, I am suddenly transported to a different place, many years ago.

I'm sitting on the lower level of a three level bunk bed, all the way in the corner on a gray rag blanket and watching my mother, as she tries with a trembling hand to light a candle on a fir branch. But the flame of her match flickers too much and does not light the candle. Finally, with my stepfather's help, the candle is lit and we three watch the slightly swaying light as one of the world's miracles. And it is so, since this one small flame from a candle fastened to a fir branch, which is stuck in a jar on our table is not only our 1944 Christmas tree, but also an affirmation to us that we are still somehow connected to the world and its traditions.

The last four months seem like a nightmare, but reality did not permit any awakening. In the fall we left Riga, Latvia with a hope to find refuge from the Red Army, somewhere in the West, but it seems that Germany had other plans for us. Disembarking from the ship *Steuben* in Danzig (now Gadansk) several hundred of us were routed into a train with a promise to find us a "new home." Our temporary home became that train, traveling for two weeks, back and forth between Danzig and Essen in West Germany. One time we stopped on the outskirts of Dresden. The day dragged on

Ilga Winicov Harrington
Waldoboro, ME

with our fellow passengers trying to alleviate swollen legs from a week of sitting with walking on the siding. First came the rumors, then the news that bombing there had already destroyed any potential stopping place for us. Days later, now on the outskirts of Essen, we sat in a ditch next to the stopped train, and fearfully watched the burning manufacturing plants in Essen. The night was cloudy but brilliantly lit by Allied bombers' search lanterns, which to my child's eyes looked like magical chandeliers hung low above us in the night sky. However, I still found myself shivering in the circle of my mother's arms as we sat in that dank and unpleasant ditch.

Eventually, the train moved again slowly, often stopping, giving priority travel to other trains with more important baggage than these foreigners. Finally, "a new home" was found for us in Leipzig. Rumors about it had swirled already for several days, but the brutal reality became unavoidable after we stepped off the train. We were loaded up in large trucks that took us to a barracks camp, where above the gate stood the prominent sign "Arbeit macht frei." We had been delivered to a Nazi work camp. Armed guards opened and then closed the massive gate so that nobody should have any illusions about our "new home."

We got out in an open area surrounded by unkempt brown barracks. Only one building looked somewhat maintained with a glass door and wide steps. This was very likely the place for camp administrators. A sharp whistle caught our attention to face a tall, imposing grey-brown clad man, in high shiny black boots, who came through the glass doors and standing on the top step briefly addressed the new arrivals. What I understood from the adults was that the camp commandant had exhorted all to faithfully work for the Nazi war effort.

Immediately afterwards men and women were separated, directing each group of about a hundred individuals to separate entrances of a barrack opposite the administrative

Ilga Winicov Harrington
Waldoboro, ME

building. We entered a large room with a strange and unusual smell. There we encountered two nurses who demanded everyone to completely disrobe for a doctor's inspection. With no acceptable excuses, in short time we were all naked, old and young, standing in a row against the wall, each clutching their small bundle of clothes. Suddenly, two white dressed men with masks entered the room and started blowing white dust at us all from what looked like spray guns. The dust had the same smell that we had first noticed in the room. After the "dusting" one of the nurses returned to the room and explained that the DDT powder used on us was to prevent us bringing lice and bedbugs into the camp. After two weeks of train travel we were not particularly clean, but "lice"...! Many of the women in our group started crying. The following doctor's inspection was relatively superficial, although the line moved slowly and the room was cold. The doctor sat in an ample leather chair and inspected each of us head-to-toe as one would inspect livestock for purchase. It was a memorable introduction to becoming an insignificant cog in the Nazi war machinery.

After dressing, we gathered our things and went out, where we heard similar stories about what had happened to the men. Rooms were assigned to us in the brown wooden barracks. Each room had two three-tiered bunk beds, a couple of wooden chairs and a tiny table. The beds came with straw mats and a gray rag blanket. The three of us shared one room with another family. The small table at the window separated the bunk beds at each wall, thus marking half the tiny room for each family.

Our room was at the end of a long and dark corridor, next to a small kitchen room with a tiny coal stove and water spigot above a small sink, which was used by all thirty or forty barrack's inhabitants for their daily needs. Toilets were in a separate barrack for men and women and once a week there were men's or women's shower hours in a different building. The showers were in a row in an open room and while the

Ilga Winicov Harrington
Waldoboro, ME

water was warm, the room was unheated, so cleanliness required a lot of shivering in the winter. In really cold weather the guards distributed a small amount of coal for each barrack's kitchen, allowing those who still had something left from supplies carried from home to cook. My mother's experiences in World War I exile had prepared her this time to take along some non-perishable. So, during our first months in the camp we would sometimes be able cook gray Latvian dried peas with a tiny piece of slab bacon. However, it was hard to cook something for us, when many others had nothing and would go to bed hungry every night. By Christmas, even our meager supplies were gone.

So began our life in the workers camp for a metal working factory, Lager Mangold Maschinenfabrik, or more precisely our slave labor camp in Leipzig. A siren would wake everyone before six every morning. Breakfast porridge was doled out in the camp's main kitchen with chicory coffee for the adults. Immediately after that, anyone age 14 and older, both men and women left for work in the metal factory until 7 o'clock in the evening. What they manufactured in the factory I do not remember. I only know that the work was heavy and strenuous and everyone returned in the evening exhausted after a day with no rest or food, but hard physical work. The evening meal in the main kitchen, therefore, was usually quiet and rarely anyone had energy to complain about the daily kohlrabi or green pea ("green wonder") soup. Together with a chunk of bread, this was daily dinner. Sometimes the "green wonder" sported something that looked like dumplings. Several of the young boys my age would then whisper that those were drowned rats, which of course spoiled my appetite completely.

However, this was Christmas Eve and the guards had handed out an extra ration of bread as we left the hall after dinner. Shivering in the sharp wind we hurried along the dark path back to our room where we found ourselves alone, since the other family was spending the evening with friends.

Ilga Winicov Harrington
Waldoboro, ME

Stepfather Arturs had somehow managed to find a fir branch and had fashioned a wire candle holder, so that we would have at least a semblance of a Christmas tree.

Now the small flame of the lit candle which reflected in the window and it's warmth absorbed all our attention. For a moment we forgot the gray passage of days only lit by the bare faint light bulb at the ceiling. Mother must have been remembering other Christmases for she suddenly asked me to recite a poem, as was our custom to do for children on Christmas Eve back at home. I had not learned anything new recently, so I started Poruks "White snow falls so lightly, on firs." After that, Mother started to sing with a tremulous voice, "Silent night, holy night" and Arturs and I joined in. Hard to say now whether we hoped that old customs would lead us back into a more normal life, or it was just the feeling of sanctity of the special night.

But children also have less lofty and more mundane thoughts. Memories of Christmas presents from previous years kept sneaking into my head, even as I knew that this year and place were different. But exceptional miracles occur in the most unlikely places. After the singing, Mother lifted the corner of the blanket on her bed and took out a small package wrapped in newspaper.

"This was left for you earlier tonight by Father Christmas," she said as she exchanged a small smile with my stepfather.

I said: "Thank you!" and with impatient fingers opened the string on the small package. In the newspaper wrapping sat a small notebook and a pencil. I swallowed and repeated: "Thank you. Thank you," turning the white pages. Even writing implements had become precious and unattainable in our circumstances.

"Father Christmas must have known that you like to write, copy poems and other things," said Mother still smiling.

Stepfather on the other hand had more practical things

Ilga Winicov Harrington
Waldoboro, ME

on his mind. "I think that we still have just a little bacon fat from cooking that last piece of bacon from home. We should spread it on our 'gift' bread from the guards and have a feast."

The small bacon fat jar was quickly found and we feasted with black bread spread with a thin layer of fat. It is was not roast goose, not a chop, not even meatloaf, but after the daily thin kohlrabi stew, it tasted magnificent.

"MMM..." said Arturs licking his upper lip, "just close your eyes and if we had a small piece of garlic, we could imagine we are eating a delicious salami sandwich."

After that I sat on Mother's lower bunk in the bed with my new little notebook and felt momentarily bewitched. Words were beginning to chase each other in my head and in my imagination I was traveling warmly wrapped in a large sled through a snow-covered deep fir forest. There was great silence and quiet peace in that mystical ride with no fear of the next bend in the road.

My first poem was written in that notebook that Christmas Eve. Unfortunately, it was lost in time, but the memories of that evening will always stay indelible, wrapped in the light of one small candle.

***

Thomas Peter Bennett
Bradenton, FL

No Return

In time and space,
flights and lives
have points
of no return.

Gregg Mosson
Baltimore, MD

Truro Dune Harmony

Blackjays with orange-hinged wings
   swoop across a dune marsh
as dusk deepens to begin:

August's zillion azure miles
   tingle above the bending coastline,
while the sunset, blocked by dunecliffs,
   hues the northern sky in tiers:

This horizon-wall, tone after tone,
   peaks and drains in bars of color,
a tuning of radiances for hours
   from a treasure horde older than humans.

A brown-and-white bespotted gull,
   as I walk past below a dunecliff, back to the hostel,
cues for its moment to nest.

***

Bill Eberle
Thomaston, ME

lilac stroke

heart attack, stroke, accident
human toll

for lilacs
heavy clinging
snow

Robert B. Moreland
Pleasant Prairie, WI

After

The crisp chill of fall in the predawn darkness
causes him to zip up the windbreaker,
walk with purpose as he makes his way out
onto the third concrete breakwater extending
into the dark water of the great lake.
He closes his eyes, breathing in time
with the waves gently lapping the shore.

Pale first light in the east hints at the day
to come. Oddly, his nightmare had begun
with a physical to go to Boy Scout camp,
his aging Italian practitioner
requesting he see a specialist who
in turn wanted to biopsy. This won't hurt.
It did. Eight weeks ago, the phone call came.

The doctor was so abrupt, not abnormal cells,
not we need to discuss. But it's cancer.
How final! Cancer! You just don't say that!
He readies for the surgery to come,
watching one last sunrise on the great lake.

Robert B. Moreland
Pleasant Prairie, WI

The day is perfect. Black night fades to blue.
As the light grows, pinks swell in crescendo
to richest oranges and deepest reds;
he draws his lungs full of air until it hurts,
savoring. Then it comes, tiny pinprick
of bright light growing to a fingernail
and bright orb birthing from the horizon,
day in full glory. Except for a pair
of seagulls searching for a morning meal,
he is alone with his thoughts. And alone
he will go to see the surgeon who will
remove that malignancy growing inside.

Life so long taken for granted focuses
not unlike that pinprick of brilliant light.
Silently he thanks God for this superb day
as he walks back to his lakeside cottage
where the fresh brew of morning awaits.

Zibette Dean
Edgecomb, ME

Gleaner

This November's wild early snowstorm
upended any foreign trees like lilacs or
apples that don't know when to drop their leaves,
tossed the Norway maple north of the house
into the road and took out the power line.
The DOT cut the tree into cord lengths.
I dragged some to the woodpile; the rest
got buried under the next plowbank.

Yesterday's rain washed away the snow.
I woke in the night to hear wood clunk on metal
Somebody's taken home a load of stove wood.

If he'd asked me I'd have given it to him.

***

Perspective

Driving East on U. S. 1,
off-season in Maine,
I shut off the radio and *pay attention*.
The road turns right, swings left,
I climb hills, coast down.
Tires sizzle on wet asphalt,
the passenger door rattles.
Flat-top asters shake white tassels
along road edges;
phone poles with their cross-trees march along,
appearing to shrink and bunch together,
and spruces poke spiky antennas
against a bright sky.

the late Carol Kramer
NY, NY

Anatomy of a Repast

Traveling in any French city has its challenges, not the least of which is speaking and understanding the language. But ah, then there is the food. After a brutally bad meal on our first night in Quebec, I was promised an elegant dinner at a fine restaurant. Arthur is not a fan of French cooking, but I am up for tasting any dish that I would not take the time and energy to prepare myself.

So, we strolled to L'Utopie a restaurant that bills its cuisine as French/Fusion. The décor is interesting, with birch tree trunks serving as the room dividers and huge faux-nature paintings adorning the walls. It's Thanksgiving eve in Canada, so the restaurant is not busy, which means we can expect great service. Jacques, who is a dead ringer for Steve Martin escorts us to a cozy table for two...let the laughs begin!!! We convince ourselves that the "Menu Bouteille" is the way to indulge and re-celebrate my 60th birthday which has been celebrated so many times that I feel like I am 65 (no complaints!).

Each of the five courses is matched to the wine which happens to be "Pinot Noir." One of our favorites as we reminisce about the movie *Sideways* and prepare ourselves for the feast to commence. The wine arrives along with some bread. I am holding back on the bread anticipating lots of good food to follow....the clock is ticking and the second serving of bread arrives. Hurray...here comes the first course..swordfish the size of a quarter (either Canadian or American) served with a red stripe. The red stripe is the vegetable, which is beet juice. The chef drew the red line on a plate that was the size of an oversized serving platter. Both the swordfish and the stripe looked lonely. After ten minutes of description, in English with a charming accent, of what we are about to eat, we finish the first course in a record 70 sec-

the late Carol Kramer
NY, NY

onds. A little perplexed, we continue to anxiously await the main meal as we are now starving. The second course is a single sea scallop served on orzo with two leaves from a brussel sprout. We are now getting drowsy from the wine and the waiting. Arthur and I love each other dearly, but we are both staring longingly in the direction of Jacques who, by the way, is no comedian like Steve Martin! In fact, he takes himself and this cuisine much too seriously. The main course finally arrives followed by a lengthy description. I, for one, have never eaten "beef cheek" and probably never will again. I decided to call it brisket due to the texture and the fact that I didn't really want to be chewing on "beef cheek." And why did they have to serve me the whole cheek with only three leaves of wilted spinach? Don't they know I love vegetables!!!

We are now approaching three hours in French/Fusion hell when the next two courses of dessert appear. I recognize the taste of ice cream but what is that froth next to it? Ahh...it's a mousse of lime and juniper, but it vaporizes on the spoon before it gets to my mouth...dessert meltdown perhaps. Arthur and I stare at each other in amazement as hunger gnaws in our guts. His tired face is quickly approaching his plate as we are left waiting for the check. Jacques (what a coward) sends his helper with l'addition which cuts a swath in our bank account. I thank my husband for his endurance and another birthday "dinner," as we vow to eat fruits & vegetables for the rest of the trip. We return to the auberge four hours later, stomachs growling, but with smiles on our faces!

Thomas Peter Bennett
Bradenton, FL

Rain Pastoral

Late afternoon
in summer,
        after the rain—
        the applause of silence.

Tree trunks and moist air
are copper,
        all else is green—
        leaves, grass, and ferns.

A primitive scene,
        with the rain scent
        and the distant thunder.

***

Transfiguration

Wedge-shaped shells
of live coquinas
transformed after death
by tide and time,
sand, and surf,
into
butterfly shells.

Janet N. Gold
Camden, ME

April in Maine

Sometimes I want nothing
but to stand boot-deep in spring mud,
to poke around the flower beds
in the chill April air,
to listen to
this heaving subterranean
gardener at work
on the seasonal meanings
of seeds and bulbs and roots
and the wordless awakenings
and the perfect beginnings of things.

I cry easily these days,
sleep lightly.

Has life always been this sweet?

Or is it because it is barely spring
and through the cold rain and salt,
in the most improbable
and in some of the desired
places hard green shoots
the tough bulbs of April in Maine
are finding their way back?

Janet N. Gold
Camden, ME

I remember, watching them,
the long nights spent waiting,
the despair that comes
from living
where things really die,
where one need not feign surprise
that tender-lipped violets
are resurrected
from the frozen land.

The garden is ragged with
crumpled leaf heaps
and straw mulch pushed aside by
the rubber knights of tulips
the spongey knives of narcissus.

The accumulation of cycles
looks in April like unmeshed gears
and broken bones.
In May it seems to work as if effortlessly,
like things that are never resolved
because they work,
work together,
have never stopped working.

Karyn Lie-Nielsen
Waldoboro, ME

Brushing Kate's Hair

My daughter, Kate, has long honey-colored hair.
Kate's hair is thick and weighty.
Around the edges are loose, whispering threads
standing out new and innocent,
younger than the wise heaviness
that hangs down her back.

When she was born she hadn't anything
to brag about. Certainly not hair.
She was curious and naked,
bald as the new moon.
My fingers would smooth the down
of her newborn roundness.
Funny nose and no hair.
A daughter with no hair.

But in the night blonde curls came.
Intuitively I continued to stroke
the bit of silk, twirling those fine threads,
weaving them through the loom of my fingers.
Promise was there.

My own hair is cut short like dried hay.
My mother's is like curled barbed wire.
But my daughter, Kate, has long honey-colored hair.

Jean Lawrence
Waldoboro, ME

Sixty-five Years Ago and Still a Fresh Memory

The sun was shining through the windows of our sixth grade classroom on the upper floor of the Wickford Academy three days after Easter in 1950. Mrs. Emma Allen, our history teacher, was up at the front of the room expounding on a topic about which we had read in our Ancient History text, when everyone heard the rustle of cellophane. She stopped talking and looked out at us. All was quiet. She picked up her chalk, and in her beautiful Palmer Method handwriting, proceeded to write our assignment on the blackboard. As soon as she turned her back, we heard it again, more rustling of cellophane.

Mrs. Allen, while not right out of college, was a new member of the Grade Six teaching team. In the fall, she had come to her teaching position after having raised her two sons to the point where they were in school and she could teach. She was a mild mannered soul, not given to ultimatums. Her lack of classroom experience didn't matter much to us; she knew her stuff and made the study of history fun. But on the day in question, her lack of a backlog of experiences with classroom antics certainly showed, and we all recognized that she had never encountered rustling such as we were hearing in our classroom.

As we started our writing, and she moved through the rows of desks offering assistance to those requiring it, all seemed quiet and everyone appeared to be diligently working the assignment. Then we heard her words:

"Blair McDonough, what are you doing?"

At first, quiet prevailed for a few seconds, then, "Eating a jelly bean," was Blair's reply.

"Whatever made you think you could snack on candy during class? You know eating candy in class is not allowed. Besides, it is very bad manners to eat in front of others if you

Jean Lawrence
Waldoboro, ME

don't have enough to share!" she offered.

Now, such words in those long gone days were supposed to bring immediate shame to the culprit, but Blair earnestly replied, "Oh, Mrs. Allen, I've got lots of beans, a whole bag full of them!"

He held up what appeared to most of us to be an extra-large bag of candy. Well, don't you think we didn't sit up and begin to pay close attention to the back and forth conversation that was going on before us?

Caught by surprise, Mrs. Allen paused, took a deep breath and said, "Well, come up here to the front of the room and let me see what you have."

After perusing the good-sized bag which Blair offered, she pronounced, "I see you do have plenty, so give everyone in the class three pieces of candy, and we'll all enjoy your treasure."

It would appear that this was a knee-jerk order that was supposed to diminish the amount of candy in the offending bag.

Assignment forgotten, we all watched with anticipation as tow-headed Blair, grinning ear to ear, walked up and down the aisles and put three jelly beans on each student's desk and then proceeded back to Mrs. Allen. She looked at the still bulging bag and suggested with a scowl that he repeat the action and give each one of us two more beans.

When he finally finished doling out the jelly beans, she took the bag and said, "I'll see you after school, and you can stay until you finish what's left."

"But, I can't," he protested.

"Of course you can; you're a walker not a bus student, so you can stay and eat your fill," she replied.

"I can't," he repeated with real conviction, his reddening face showing his predicament.

"Why not?" she asked.

Silence prevailed while he thought, and then came his reply, "I only like the black ones!!!"

Jean Lawrence
Waldoboro, ME

With that pronouncement, the entire class dissolved into "behind the hands" snickers.

At that point not only Mrs. Allen but also the class knew that the attempt at decisive discipline action was lost. She took a deep breath, looked at Blair and then at all of us who were intent on munching on our jelly beans, smiled weakly, sighed, and replied, "We'll see!"

I'm sure Blair picked up his beans after school, but whether he had to eat all of them in one sitting, we never heard. Was this the only antic that Blair pulled during our twelve years of schooling? By no means! Never a real discipline case, he sure did add a flair for the unexpected, no matter what the class or the grade. In today's education system, he would be classified as gifted and talented, for he learned his lessons very quickly and was way ahead of most of us when it came to inquisitiveness and creativity.

Over the past 65 years, Blair, along with the rest of us in his class, learned to taste all the colored jelly bean experiences that life has given us. He had many black jelly bean, joy-filled times over the years, and many of them were shared with us in school and at reunions. Just as his jelly bean clash with our teacher taught us to keep our Easter basket goodies at home, it also pointed out the fact that breaking a rule can, in some situations, provide entertainment and enjoyment for more than the culprit.

F. Anthony D'Alessandro
Celebration, FL

Darned Dublin Granddad

I glared at the granddad, twisted like a frail willow tree in a
    Florida hurricane.
He donned his sporty and patched Sam Snead flat cap. I
    sneered.
The gap-toothed, snowy head playfully ruffled his grandkids'
    hair. One boy shared granddad's
goal post toothed look, the other, about two spins of the
    calendar older, flaunted Hollywood teeth
neatly threaded in place, like a well-woven white picket
    fence.
On the steps of a swarming store, sandwiched between a row
    of buildings in downtown Dublin,
ivory brows amused his grandsons. He rolled a freckled ball
    across the scrawny storefront road.
On a street barely wider than a back alley, older boy casually
    kicked the creased, hissing ball.
They pranced and punted on and on.
Waiting for my bride to end vital shoe purchasing, I saw this
    play during a worker's lunch shift.
Dublin granddad jousted with his boys, then pointed to his
    wrist. His watch dictated departure.
My grandboys in the tropics, across the Big Pond came to
    mind.
The winds of summer blew us apart. I remembered our
    baseball tosses before my leaving.
I'd amused them with my tattered baseball cap and relived
    the last time I'd mussed their manes.
What were my little buddies doing without me? I imagined
    them side-by-side with the Dubliners.
My two, blued eyed and straw headed like many Dubliners,
    his two sported ginger locks.

(continued)

F. Anthony D'Alessandro
Celebration, FL

Love, not rage incited my pining heart to react jealously to
    the absence of my buddies,
currently stateside bound, while Dublin Granddad had his
nearby, leaping, and laughing.
Perhaps I didn't dislike Dublin granddad at all.
Perhaps he merely represented a tottering, living reminder of
    what I missed at that moment.
Perhaps the time was ripe for me to listen to my summons
    and soar across the stormy Atlantic,
and to reunite with my own grandsons.

***

Steve Troyanovich
Florence, NJ

Something of an Irish Poem
for Therese

may leprechauns always
watch over you
while the warm rays
of their rainbows
forever light
your path...
where love is born
each day
filling your world
with dream gardens
and wishing wells
beyond all time...

Tom Adamson
Fremont, NE

My First Breath Back

Wide open rolling skies,
Wide open blue-born day.
Not sure how or why
But I finally got away.

In the city of lightning
The skies are never calm.
Got blood on my bones,
Sweat on my palm.
So much time has slipped by—
Seems I long ago lost track.
But I'm finally home again—
My first breath back.

      I've wandered the sacred fields.
      Stormy eyes followed my every move.
      Long ago I wrote on the ancient caves.
      Now I've got nothing left to prove.

Got an appointment in Samarra.
People will dance and sing.
They'll line up, dozens-deep,
Smile and kiss my ring.
So much time has bled to dust,
Miles rolled out on the track.
But I'm finally home again—
My first breath back.

Edie Schmoll
Menifee, CA

Memories of Mom

This one's for you, Mom!

My mother will become 100 years old shortly, so I decided to let her know how much she has done to enrich my life, and that I think she is a wonderful person.

I watched my mom as she lost two husbands and carried on with dignity and courage. My dad died suddenly when I was nine years old, leaving her with three young children, a new baby, and very little income.

Although my mother never hugged or kissed me, I knew for a certainty that I was loved. My brothers and I were never hungry, cold, or ill-treated.

We were taught to respect adults, and everyone else's rights; never to lie or cheat or steal; to do our chores without complaint; and to put forth our best efforts every day at school. There was no reward for making the honor roll—it was expected. Homework was done without parental help, and turned in when due.

No one had time to read to us or tuck us in at night; but my mom showed her love with a clean and comfortable home, by keeping us well-fed and clothed, and doing the best she could. We understood this.

She gave each of us a dime to go to the movies on Sundays, and sometimes even an extra penny for candy!

We had holes in our shoes, but *never in our hearts.*

Yes, I felt loved when I was a child. And it was my beautiful mother who showed us how to love—and how to live—by her luminous example.

Laureen Haben, OSF
Milwaukee, WI

Poised

Backstage
waiting patiently
trees still flaunt
their flora of green.

Alert
for the master's baton
signaling autumn equinox
a cantata of orange and red.

***

Belva Ann Prycel
Alna, ME

Springtime Harbor

Sun-bedazzled, crystal mornings,
Wing-tips over wave and sea;
Prophesies of days alluring
Poppies, flowered pageantry.

Glad we walk as waters meet
Mudflat's dark dominion wide;
Shellfish geysers splash our feet,
Grass in racklines mark the tide.

Melodies of spring surround us,
Music of the wakening seas;
On the harbor, jewels astound us,
Flashing diamond symphonies.

Eileen Hugo
Spruce Head, ME & Stoneham, MA

Monhegan

Island time is gentle, slow, we dillydally, dream,
pen poems about cliffs, birds and sea surround.
A rainy day we greet with no surprise and no regret
It pulls us closer to the warmth of stories yet to tell.

Flocks of cedar waxwings twitter in tumbles of brush
roused by risk or chance, flare up, a burst cinnamon.
A lone painter streaks sunset across the canvas
his sea is wide, darkest gray, stuttered with curls of white.

Atop the headland and as far as eye could see
pure sky in the offing, atop a chop splattered sea.
Paths lead down, fairy house on the way wild flowers
        abound.
A chorus of meadow bobolink trill Monhegan's song.

***

Chickens

Hen in the pen.
Idling near the water
Checking out the rooster
Kicking up the hay
Fluttering to the coop
Nighttime calling
Sleeping on the roost until the break of day

Sally Woolf-Wade
New Harbor, ME

Deadly Conflict

The Battle of the Boxer and the Enterprise
September 5, 1813

We are two hundred years too late
to witness the conflict out on the bay:
the fight of the *Boxer* and *Enterprise*,
the smoke that billowed into the sky.
We stand here now on the point of land
once named by the natives *Pemaquid*.
Safe on shore the onlookers stood
hearing explosions, breathing the smoke,
not sure what the bloodshed was all about.
Those who watched, knew nothing of reasons,
were drawn to the shore by the smell of danger.
They did not know that, at age twenty-seven,
this was the captain's first commission.
Blyth nailed his colors to *Boxer's* mast,
Burrows maneuvered *Enterprise* alongside,
moved nine-pounders from bow to stern,
and two young captains too young to die
ordered the carronades to fire.
Boxer suffered the first of the broadsides.
Her topgallants shredded, exploded in flames,
her main topmast was split into pieces,
tons of sail and spars thundered down.
Crippled, the *Boxer* could not change her course.
A cannonball sliced Captain Blyth in two.
A musketshot pierced Captain Burrows' hip.
He sat dying on the *Enterprise* deck,
refused to accept Britain's sword of honor,
ordered it to Blyth's home be sent.
Burrows' final words, *I die content.*
On Munjoy Hill, the captains lie,
two brave young men too young to die.

Celine Rose Mariotti
Shelton, CT

They Called Him Up Yonder

In Memory of

My Dad, Peter J. Mariotti

June 29, 1931–May 9, 2011

Dressed in their ponchos to protect them from the pouring rain, Paul, Joey, Willie and Stanley marched through the rice fields and mud of South Korea, outside of Taegu. Korea is a cold country, so cold that some of the soldiers were found frozen sitting on the ground with guns in their hands.

Joey carried the radio and Stanley had the full field pack, and Paul carried their rations and kept a lookout for the enemy. As it was growing dark, they stopped to take a rest and took out their rations of powdered eggs and baked beans and their canteens filled with water. Paul ate it because he was hungry but he thought about his mom's good Italian cooking. He missed eating the polenta and the pasta. He missed his friends that he grew up with and hung around with all the time at their favorite drugstore on the corner. They all stopped for milkshakes or ice cream sodas there. Old Man Lester who ran the drugstore knew all the kids well and even would lend them money when they needed it.

While Paul ate he listened to his friend Willie play the harmonica and he remarked, "I wonder what my mom is doing right now."

"I wonder what my mom and my sister are doing," Willie chimed in.

"I bet my girlfriend is knitting me a sweater," said Joey.

"I bet my mom is making some pierogies, " Stanley added.

"Sure hope this war is over soon," said Paul.

"Me, too. I just want to go home," replied Willie and he

Celine Rose Mariotti
Shelton, CT

started playing "Chattanooga Chu-Chu" on his harmonica.

"I love Glen Miller," said Paul.

"Me too," exclaimed Joey, "my girlfriend and I always dance to his music."

Stanley motioned that they had to get moving. "I think I see the North Koreans just over the ridge there," he whispered.

"Okay, let's go."

The four of them marched with their gear, hoping to meet up with the rest of their unit. Somehow they had all been separated. The night sky lit up with flashes of artillery. Paul said a prayer to himself as they marched along.

"Watch out for the mines, guys," warned Willie, shining his flashlight as they walked along. They heard American voices up on the hill and spotted Ralph and George. They were both part of their unit.

"Boy, are we glad to see you four guys!" exclaimed Ralph.

"Glad to see you too," replied Joey as they all shook hands.

"Benny got killed down by the river," said George.

"Oh, no, Benny! Geez. He was going to be a dad," sighed Paul, wiping away his tears.

They marched together, all six of them. The mud and dirt caked under their boots and the rain pelted their faces. Just as they were trudging through the woods, Joey stepped on a mine and was blown to bits. Willie took out his harmonica and played the taps.

"Poor Joey. They just called him up yonder," said Paul with tears streaming down his face.

This story is based on so many of the stories my dad told us about the Korean War. He told us that when one of his friends got killed, a fellow soldier would always blow taps on the harmonica because it meant one of their buddies was just called up yonder.

My dad, Peter J. Mariotti was a Korean War veteran. He

Celine Rose Mariotti
Shelton, CT

served in the US Army, 1st Cavalry, 7th Regiment. He fought outside Taegu and on the Pusan Perimeter. My dad always talked about it. He was in a battle outside Taegu at the end of September, 1950 and the gunfire was exploding, he got thrown and rolled down a hill and injured his back. The rest of the soldiers in the unit all were killed. He was the first from the Naugatuck Valley to be wounded in Korea and he was awarded the Purple Heart. He was also one of only two soldiers who survived that battle. My dad, like so many other Korean War veterans was a forgotten hero. But to me he will always be a hero and the best dad in the whole world.

***

Eileen Hugo
Spruce Head, ME & Stoneham, MA

Clear Cut

These trees weren't cut with a saw but squeezed by
a mechanical claw and twisted from the ground.
This was not a paper company
not poor neighbors trying to make ends meet
using the wood for their heat
not forest rangers pruning the forest
This was a profiteer.
Trucks chewed to the edges of the one lane road
gnawed next to my property line.
Trees on three sides and a road on the other.
Now I look out my windows and see carnage
I wonder what those trees were worth.

John T. Hagan
Springboro, OH

Alice Conroy*

Of Honey Baxter, glum O'Rourke laments,
As violin takes me back through the years.
Upon lost chance, the singer now comments,
While I for Alice Conroy shed my tears.
***

O'Rourke's nostalgic song has followed date
Of recent bash that rendered old friends' smiles.
To my delight, she'd flown from western state,
And she'd not lost her grace or playful wiles.

I'd found her late on that reunion night;
On arm of husband, she had brightly shown.
Suppressing longings, I tried as I might.
She had a woman from a darling grown.

In conversation, she'd remained a star.
Her beauty had not waned but just matured.
Her mirth and mind years simply could not mar.
Of my enjoyment her charms had insured.

Our meeting had rekindled my old flame.
The time and space had somehow taken flight.
A glamour girl, and Alice was her name,
And now O'Rourke sings back my squandered night.
***

She'd touched me lightly at the high school hop.
I stammered so; she may have thought me coy.
I'd known her long, but worship wouldn't stop.
Why would she talk with such a common boy?

John T. Hagan
Springboro, OH

To dance with her I positively pined.
The music played, and I talked on and on.
If I'd dared ask her, would she have declined?
Soon hop was over and my chance was gone.
***
Of Honey Baxter, sad O'Rourke now sings
And rues the time of his neglected chance.
In my two ears his mournful story rings.
I did not Alice Conroy ask to dance.

*Inspired by Dennis O'Rourke's "Honey Baxter."

***

Kate Leigh
Portsmouth, NH

Brooklyn

The carillon sounds as if it drops soft notes
From some faraway heaven, in fresh strands
This blue bright morning, as cars honk, as
Birds twitter, as the phone chimes, ahhh
Brooklyn, grace has not left thee, or good
Surprise abandoned thy side, you still hold
Diverse families, quaint local stores that if they go
Under we will miss and hold memories of,
Birded hedges, spring gardens, seen from
This six story apartment building that
Houses hundreds of individuals' stories
Inside its shabby-chic lobby and rubbishy
Elevators; we can walk everywhere from here.

Anne W. Hammond
Woolwich, ME

The Cracked Kayak

A svelte form meant to fly through the water,
The kayak has seams on her coating,
Cracks in her resin,
Where she was dragged between boulders,
Flipped over in rock gardens,
Or slammed on a ledge close to shore.
Dents radiate outward
Like a pie split by a knife,

Cracks roughen the vessel like an ancient pine chest,
A wooden table left in the rain
The wrinkles on an old face.

Is her hull solid, her form well founded?
Is her fiberglass damaged by hidden wounds?

Does the wind shove her off track?
A deluging wave start a leak?

How far is too far?

No way to tell except to run her into the water
Make for an island
Try her again somewhere out there.

Kathy McHugh
Ogunquit, ME

The Day Mom Died

The day Mom died I had just mailed out the last of the invitations to my parents' upcoming 70th anniversary. I was standing in line at the market here in Ogunquit, Maine waiting for a sandwich before leaving for work when I got the call. In my distress I was fortunate to be comforted by kind neighborhood business owners; one who held onto me, one who pulled over on Route 1 to hug me; another who offered to drive me sixty miles to the hospital. My sons were already on the way.

The day after Mom died I was resting on Dad's couch in New Hampshire. I heard his feet and cane thumping down the hall to the kitchen where he said, "Ah—coffee!" The phone rang. A school bus roared down the hill. The newspaper was delivered. There was news on the television. I could barely move. I wasn't ready for any of that. I felt like my world had stopped, just like Mom's. Couldn't it all just stop for one day in respect for her?

More calls came in. Flowers, cards and messages were delivered. Dad, my brother, his wife, my aunt and I went to the funeral home to plan Mom's services. The picture board a friend had helped design for the anniversary was displayed at the wake, as was some of Mom's quilting. My sister-in-law was surprised that I postponed the wake and funeral a few days. My brother was surprised that I accepted a minister of a different faith for Mom's funeral.

The services were beautiful. The minister played and sang Mom's favorite hymns and songs on his guitar. He told the stories of her life, mostly the humorous ones, like when Mom diligently decorated Dad's retirement cake with the Bell Telephone symbol. Then the day of the party, Dad was up on a chair taking pictures of it, fell on it, and Mom went to bed. And in the days of WWII when there was great fear that the

Kathy McHugh
Ogunquit, ME

world would come to an end, Mom and Dad were staying in a hotel room, unaware that there was a train track on the other side of the wall. The train rumbled and roared through at five in the morning, shaking them up. My sons did readings about how quilting was important to her; how life is pieced together and planned out beyond our control.

Relatives and friends from near and far visited, made us meals, took us out to honor Dad for Veterans Day, reminisced with us, laughed and cried with us. When they left I stayed. I sorted through Mom's possessions; some I gave away, some I kept. A caring friend commented, "What's the hurry? Be gentle with yourself." One friend shared with me how he coped with the loss of his mother, while another assured me that I could still talk with my mother even though she had departed, adding that it takes time to recover from grief; that it is normal.

The holidays were especially painful. I didn't decorate much. I didn't want to hear Christmas carols or buy gifts, but I saw hope in the lights. I made myself get out and tried to smile, not wanting to rob anyone of joy. One person commented, "It is my hope that you honor your mother by celebrating the holidays." I did, but in my own way, at my own pace, but filtering, limiting, some avoidance. My older son and his wife invited me to their home in Massachusetts where we exchanged gifts. They took me to a religious shrine which was beautifully decorated with colorful lights, angels and stars. I lit a candle in the chapel display in memory of Mom. My younger son and his wife in New Hampshire proudly hosted and prepared the holiday meal for the first time. I spent the day there then went to be with Dad, who decided to stay home alone for the first time in seventy years.

It's been five months since the day Mom died and I am home in Maine—back to my routine, back to writing, reading, playing piano and taking walks. My radio is on. There's coffee in my cup. I'm out and about in my town once again, visiting friends and neighbors. Spring has arrived. A new tourist sea-

Kathy McHugh
Ogunquit, ME

son is beginning. I go over to help Dad once a week or so and call him three times a day. Life went on—even mine, though I am just now realizing that Mom will never see another summer, enjoy another Mother's Day, birthday or anniversary. She won't read the paper, have a meal, watch a favorite show, answer the phone or greet me in person.

The day Mom died her daily life was disrupted and disturbed, ending quickly. She said, "I need air," then collapsed and became unresponsive after a joyful walk down the hallway of home in the middle of that Monday in November. The paramedics tried to save her, but she was already gone.

Grief is so overwhelming. It makes you feel like everything stops. Grief is different for everyone. Some of us need a little more time. I know I did. Getting my life back and enjoying it doesn't mean I've forgotten Mom—it means that her life mattered, just like mine does. And I think that's what she would have wanted....

***

Peggy Trojan
Brule, WI

Childhood Duty

when the snow melted fast
on a warm April day
we cleared ice dams
with sticks
to free the little rivers
unclogging streams
of leaves and debris
anxious to help the world
emerge into spring

Trudy Wells-Meyer
Scottsdale, AZ

What possible is. . . .

Isabel,
   happy at Edgewater Haven, to be 100 years, a mind so
clear, a smile so dear,
   adored by caregivers—life is rich with sunshine in your
heart. . . .
   Thinking of Aunt Isabel I see flowers, irises, azaleas and
lilies, an infectious smile,
   a glimpse of faith—eyes of joy; her regal air reflecting
gentleness everywhere.

Isabel,
   fell in her garden at 95 cutting grass with a weed
whacker, a momentous,
   life-changing slip. A widow living alone, moved in to the
newly built dream house
   at 85 years old, enjoying each day of days.
A Lady with an extra ordinary sense of stillness, strength,
   unconscious grace,
thinking of those long ago childhood mornings, growing up
   on a Wisconsin farm.
Winter days hard and dense, gray the color of the future,
   a more innocent time;
remembrance from the past not necessarily as they were;
   where all that love began.

Trudy Wells-Meyer
Scottsdale, AZ

Isabel,

now home is a small room, a wheelchair her best and
daily friend,

pictures on walls and dresser; endless days she claims
speed by too fast.

People there of all walks-of-life, some dementia—they
still know to smile.

The question of time, its elusiveness, as Isabel looks out
to the gray, sometimes

blue Wisconsin River across the street, her eyes can see
silence outside—safe inside.

Caregivers with happy eyes, their hue of kindness
warms the heart.

A son far away in glorious sizzling Arizona; her
daughter living near; safe indeed.

Isabel,

when she was young with hopes and desperate feelings,
her future a blaze of maybes

harboring dreams of greatness; the size being measured
by her memories as

she pretends to be a child again. Memories like random
photographs, the smell of

a summer rainstorm, the million stars seen from her
cold tiny room.

Her sisters and brothers all gone—all ten of them, her
sister Esther's 100th birthday, in Florida,

she attended at 94, her aged hand holding old pictures
close to her nose,

those centenarian eyes still able to see.

Trudy Well-Meyer
Scottsdale, AZ

Isabel,
in age she understands . . . the fountain of youth now
her fountain of wisdom:
Contentment is one of your greatest blessings . . .
Experience a brutal teacher,
losing a daughter, Janie only ten, to Polio. Now no
longer anything to fear,
no stranger to reach for the light . . . and pray.

Isabel,
with a centenarian knowledge of life, a lifetime to talk
about, she knows
precious time lasted a little longer each day back then;
the journey is the reward. . . .
A face wrinkle free, still using Oil of Olay, beauty as
evident as in youth,
for anyone to stare at, a sight of wonder for her visitors
from the West;
her sophisticated, genius nephew with a degree from
the school of life,
her brother's son, my husband for 40 magical years.

Isabel,
her room now holds her colors, her timing . . . her
heart. A gentle wave of a hand
that touched so many, today, belonged to us. We drove
away with an image
to remain etched in stone, a prayer that will carry me:
Get one thing right: that is Love.

What lies behind us and what lies before us are
tiny matters compared to what lies within us.
—Ralph Waldo Emerson

Jane Welch
Rockland, ME

How Are You? Who Am I?

"How are you?" he called in greeting.
"Who am I?" I heard him say.
Who? How?
Two words, three letters hold such meaning.
So often I'd asked myself, "Who am I?"
Did this man truly want to know?
Had I finally found someone
Who really wanted to know me?
Who would help me know myself,
Who wanted me to know him?
My heart felt warm and open;
Our eyes met and our journey began.

***

P. C. Moorehead
North Lake, WI

Gliding

I live a submarine life,
gliding the depths,
nearing the bottom.

A periscope gives me hope.
I see some light.

A vast ocean,
a vast night,
yet—hope glimmers.

Irene Zimmerman
Greenfield, WI

Leaving Green Lake

The lake's awash in shining red and gold.
Leaves sprinkle on the windshield
and through the open window.

I ease down the darkening, leaf-drenched
road along the shore, listening to
the hushed tête-à-tête of wind and trees.

Ahead, my car lights catch a fawn, motionless
in the road. It wanders off, halts again,
ears alert, looking toward the water.

Inching past the lake, muting now to gray,
I take with me the poem of fawn, still
and listening in the dying light.

***

Invitation

Come with me, friend, to see the snow
that flew like angels during the night.
We'll walk tiptoe through fields of white,
fill memory's well with starry lace.

Then when next summer's heated vise
attempts to squeeze our spirits dry,
we'll drink our fill, you and I,
from winter's overflow of grace.

Janet Morgan
Litchfield, ME

Holding It Tightly...

Holding it tightly, I froze on the spot when I heard screaming from above. A woman who looked like one of Macbeth's three witches bellowed at us from across the street. There she stood, on her doorstep, pointing a long bony finger in our direction. She *terrified* us.

Her wrath descended upon my older cousin and me. "I'm calling your parents. I know who you are, you little thieves!" she roared at us from across an otherwise peaceful country road.

My thoughts raced. *Why is it that people only know who we are when we're doing something wrong? Why can't we magically become invisible?* But what she said was true! We were thieves! That was the worst part of it. I bowed my head. I could not look at this crazy woman. *What would she do to us? Would she call our parents?*

How had this awful moment happened? Just minutes earlier we had been walking towards home on a fine spring day when Dea had piped up, "Oh, look at those beautiful wildflowers down there." Stunning bright yellow flowers rose above the stubbly grass. They waived in the wind, calling out for us to come and join them. "Let's go pick them," Dea said.

My conscientious eight-year-old mind told me to wait by the side of the road. But I wanted to go with Dea as she stepped off the graveled surface and started her descent into sin. I stood, rooted to the spot, thinking how I could justify trespassing. And then I had it: two years ago—right after we moved to Birch Point—my father had taken us to pick blueberries farther down on this same hill. He had gotten permission from the owner to go down there anytime, he had told us. We had gone there many times.

"Come on!" I heard Dea's insistent voice. So, with justification in hand, I went. "Wildflowers belong to everyone," Dea

Janet Morgan
Litchfield, ME

called back over her shoulder as she picked one, two, three flowers. I ran towards her, stopped by her side, and reached out. I had just wrapped my fingers around a long stem when the yelling had begun. My hand jerked the flower upward. Looking down, I expected to see roots hanging off the end of the stem. What I saw, however, was a crudely ripped stem dangling from beneath my closed fist.

"What do you think you're doing with my daffodils?" The woman was old, *very* old. She must have been at least 60, with that wild black and gray-streaked hair stiffly swirling around her ancient-to-us head.

The daffodil, as I now knew it to be, was being crushed in my hand as my fingers convulsed into a tight knot. "Bring them to me! Bring them here right now!" That awful voice had me petrified. Dea and I looked at one another. I could tell from the look on Dea's face that we shared the same thought: *Could we get away if we made a break for it? After all, she was old and probably couldn't run very fast.*

But the woman knew who we were, or so she said. We couldn't take the chance. We hung our heads in defeat as we trudged what seemed like a mile up to her front doorstep. Standing as far away from her as our short arms would allow, we reached out and placed the flowers into the old woman's outstretched claw. We stepped back quickly. The house was old also; it was also decrepit. It horrified us. Would she snatch us up, like the crone in Hansel and Gretel had done? Instead the door slammed in our faces just as we thought we were goners. We didn't have to be told twice to scram.

Back in our separate homes, we waited for punishment to descend. We waited for weeks. Were our parents making us suffer by ignoring the incident until we felt safe once again? Miraculously nothing ever happened; our day of reckoning never came. Or perhaps we had exacted our own punishment.

Later that summer when the blueberries ripened, I

Janet Morgan
Litchfield, ME

stayed home. I could not risk seeing the old woman and having her follow through on her threat. I invented an illness when my parents and brother went back to the field of infamy for *their* reward.

***

P. C. Moorehead
North Lake, WI

The Force of the Wave

The force of the missing is like a wave.
It comes into shore, crashing against me.
It is a punishing, punishing wave.

"Surf's up," I say, as the feeling
forces its way through me.
Being light does not help.
This is a punishing wave.

"Get the surfboard," I say, "and ride it out."
From experience, I know the force will abate,
and, from experience, I know the force will return.

How much good is a life's experience?
Not much—and everything.
I can handle this; I've done it before.
The surf breaks, but I don't.

Steve Troyanovich
Florence, NJ

your orange bears...

for Kenneth Patchen

"Put your hands in mine. We will seek God together."
   And I answered,
   "It is your father who is lost, not mine."
   Then the sky filled with tears of blood, and snakes sang.
                   —Kenneth Patchen

trying to hunt down
your orange bears hunters still stalk
the bleeding tracks of the last
winter wolf...   wounded shrouds
of lost wars drag on...

no longer content to murder only men
these same sporting pimps
heap bodies of faceless children
torn from nameless mothers
upon their digital altars
mouthing solemn paeans
to cyber gods...

rites of darkness fill seared landscapes
ripped from this most ancient star
where heroes rot below nocturnal temples and
concealed gates awaiting entry into more
forgotten edens...

still *the stars go to sleep so peacefully*
stay by my side like a child
seeking that special rainbow in a haymow
where no one bleeds or is orphaned
or remains dreamless anywhere
on this gentle earth...

Ellen Sander
Belfast, ME

transition

a grey crab in a
west moving cloud
reaches for the sun

today the icicle,
glistening taper of descent
weeps

its tears
fall past my window
moisten buried seeds

***

Winter Moon

Winter moon so
Luminous on fresh snow
Pours through the slats
In silken blue, and
stripes this poem

Michelle M. Faith
Camden, ME

Night Watch

for Jim and June Young

"Call us if you see anything,"
we admonish, sending forth expeditions
from our supper table.

In other years we drew up lawn chairs
to keep vigil for the first sliver
of yellow bursting the green skin.

This year, though, through a haze
of cinnamon coffee and raspberry birthday pie,
we startle to hear the children scream
"Primroses! Primroses!"
and rush to the flower bed to gawk
at after-births, hoping secretly,
perhaps, for instant replay.

Neighbors, phoned, drive up.
"Ah well," one says, "we can just stand
and watch the beauty."

We do. We do, leaning close.
Two evening primroses, petals folded back
upon themselves, shiver nakedly
before us, opening as if
some unknown urge has moved them
toward this one ecstatic night.

Like Peter, I long to say I watched
with them through their swift and silent prayer.
Like him, I say in my heart:
I will be with you your whole life long.

Michelle M. Faith
Camden, ME

We go about our business, though,
and the neighbors drive off.
"Maybe another time," they say
of the few tiny buds not ready yet
to bloom elusively toward death.

Tomorrow, with the first touch of dawn,
these two will be gone.
For now, I gladly praise them
for their singleness—
their brief quiver of light
within the holy dark.

***

Steve Troyanovich
Florence, NJ

Tipasa

for Albert Camus

in the last solitude
the wind
sang to the sea
cradled in dream
fearful of wakening
that final melancholy
of memory...

how cold the earth
how warm the sky
without reprieve
the peace of stones

Susan Gerry
Friendship, ME

Perspective

Looking down on the island from the cliffs above the cove
I see two dozen cellar holes, granite foundations
      surrounded by lilacs
gone wild.

Wide granite steps to nowhere, where houses once stood,
where children were born and old people died.

An apple orchard with sad, fallen branches, its trees too old
      to bear fruit.
A cemetery full of simple granite markers.

Passing clouds spread patches of shade in rhythmic
      patterns that connect the
island and the ocean to the mainland. Everything is
      connected. Everything
happens for a reason.

Knowing that a whole village and a towering forest lived and
died in that four-mile length of island pulls my life into per-
spective.

Gin Mackey
Owls Head, ME

Queen for a Day

On the day in question, we all arrived home from a week's vacation at the same time. My husband Dick and I returned from Bar Harbor, Maine, and our daughter Ashley from Cape Cod. Ashley had graduated from high school the week before, and was tickled about her first vacation with friends, sans parents. We shared our vacation adventures.

Then the real world intruded in the form of laundry, lots of it. Dick and Ashley planned to leave the next day on another vacation. Sailing on the coast of Maine would be Ashley's last hurrah before starting two summer jobs to earn money for her first year at Wellesley College. While Ashley chatted with friends on the phone, I threw a load of Dick's and my laundry into the washer, then put it in the dryer. I came back later to see if it was dry. It wasn't, not quite, so I closed the door and hit the button to restart the drying.

But instead of tumbling clothes, what I heard was a faint humming. I kept opening and closing the dryer and pushing the button. I kept getting a faint hum. Naturally, Dick then had to do the same thing, opening and closing, opening and closing, poking the button. Nothing.

As we all know, the definition of insanity is doing the same thing over and over again, and expecting different results. I glanced out the window. It was dark. I expected the men in white coats would wait until morning now to come for us.

In desperation, we started doing the things that people do to try to fix something. We reset the circuit breakers, opened and closed and poked. We opened the door, but this time removed some of the clothes from the dryer, then closed and poked some more. We muscled the dryer out from its place against the wall. This was accompanied by a deafening screaming of metal on the concrete basement floor, which I

Gin Mackey
Owls Head, ME

found somehow satisfying, almost as if by torturing the thing it might finally see things my way. On some level, I suppose, I was hoping that activity, noise and grunting would equate to progress.

We peered at the backside of the dryer, discussed it, looked at it some more, harder this time. We didn't actually do anything to the dryer, but because we had looked, we felt compelled to open and close and poke it, just in case a harsh glare had had some effect. The only effect appeared not to be on the dryer, which remained staunchly the same, but on my back, where I now felt a stabbing pain.

We waited a while, watched a couple of innings of the Red Sox, and went back to the dryer. At this point we were fantasizing that the dryer had simply overheated and would be fine after cooling down. Open, close, poke.

Nothin'.

I had a psychology background. I realized we were in the denial phase of dealing with appliance breakdowns. The things we were doing were our way of giving ourselves time to adjust to the eventuality of losing our beloved dryer. We had to move to the next phase.

"It's busted," I said to Dick.

He pursed his lips.

I could see he needed more time.

"There's gotta be a reset button somewhere," he said. "Darn thing"—I'm paraphrasing here—"just needs to be reset."

A reset button didn't magically appear, reach out and grab us. We shared the conviction that actually applying tools to an appliance was akin to a death wish, accompanied by about a ninety percent chance of fatality by electrocution.

"I'll call the repair guy," I said. Upon reflection, I realized we were upholding one of the laws of the universe, one as old and true as Murphy's Law. The law is as follows: if an appliance is going to break down, it will occur on a Friday night, the start of the longest period of time in the week when the repair guy is unavailable.

On the bright side, Monday wasn't a holiday.

As I folded the somewhat damp laundry, I realized I didn't feel as badly about it as I might. After all, Dick was going sailing, so his clothes were going to get soggy anyway. I was just getting a jump on things for him. As Ashley put her clothes in the washing machine, we remembered that there was a dryer at the club where we moored the sailboat. She could dry her clothes there while she and her dad got the *Carpe Diem* shipshape for a week of sailing.

Monday, I called the repair guy and described the problem.

"The motor's gone."

Dollar signs—lots of them—danced before my eyes. "Are you sure?"

He apparently picked up on the slight note of hysteria in my voice. "Bring the phone over by the dryer and let me listen."

I was upstairs, the dryer was downstairs. The cord was long. It was worth a try. I started down the stairs. By stretching each and every coil in the cord to its full length, I could get close to the dryer. By fully extending my arms, I could hold the phone in my left hand and poke the dryer with my right. I poked it; he listened.

"Yup, the motor's gone," he said again. "Factoring in the price of the motor and labor, it's gonna cost you two hundred dollars to get it fixed. It's time to get a new dryer."

"Could you come over and look at it anyway? Just in case it's something else?" It dawned on me that it was supposed to be the other way around. The repair guy was supposed to want to charge me for coming over and looking at the appliance and then making costly repairs even when he knew it was hopeless. My job was to say, forget it, we need a new dryer.

He could come tomorrow at two o'clock.

He did.

Gin Mackey
Owls Head, ME

It was the motor.

The repair guy, Mr. Thibodeau, had worked on our stove a few months earlier. He was a reasonable man, fair, and I trusted him. I asked him about brands of dryers. He recommended a Kitchen Aid, the kind he bought for himself. He looked behind the dryer. "Tell them to replace the venting, too."

He then opened up the washing machine, because, well, that's what he does. It was an old Maytag. He noted that it had its original motor, somewhere around twenty-five years old and still kicking. But he looked for rust, and found some. At this point, we were down on our hands and knees, looking up at the tub part of the washer.

"See that little rust spot? I could put my pen right through there. Some time or other it will give way and you'll have a flood in here."

I knew he was right. My husband and I had talked numerous times about how we were on borrowed time with the washer. Mr. T recommended that I think seriously about also getting a new washer.

I was a pushover. An expert in the business had just convinced me that we really, really needed to get a brand new washer and a brand new dryer. I had to do it, for the good of the family. My husband was on vacation; there was no need to worry him with the details. An image of a Christmas tree popped into my head. Was this the fabled Christmas in July I'd long heard talked about?

"Get the LAT2500. It's pretty much the same one you have here. They've been making them for forty-five years. People love 'em."

I scribbled down his recommendations.

The cost of the visit was thirty dollars. Pretty cheap for lots of great advice from a knowledgeable source. I had dreaded the process of researching appliances, comparing prices, making sure I got a good value. Now I wouldn't have to.

Gin Mackey
Owls Head, ME

I called the appliance store where we had bought our stove. To my amazement, I could order both appliances over the phone and have them delivered in two days time. How convenient. Kenny the salesperson confirmed that the appliances I purchased were bestsellers, great values. He told me the moving company would call me the next day and give me a three-hour window during which they would deliver my appliances on Thursday.

I cringed. So far it had been easy. But delivery people were notoriously unreliable. Everyone knew that. The next day they called. They'd be at my house between ten and one on Thursday.

Right.

Thursday morning at ten, I started moving the paraphernalia that would impede getting the old appliances out and the new ones in. I didn't feel like I had to rush. I'd be lucky if they showed up that day at all, maybe that week. After clearing the way, I got the broom and swept the floor. The doorbell rang.

No, couldn't be.

It was. I showed the mover where the new appliances would go. He quickly unhooked the existing washer and dryer. He left, and a few minutes later came back in. A second man followed, holding a thick strap, which he positioned around the washer. While he lifted with the strap, the other man lifted with his hands. Without benefit of a dolly, they picked up the washer and walked out with it as if it were made of cardboard. Moments later, using the same method, they walked in with the new washer. In a few minutes, it was attached and functioning. They repeated the process with the dryer.

"You're awesome," I said. "I don't know how you could have made it any easier." I thought about it for a second, then laughed. "Unless you did the first load of laundry for me."

They politely declined.

Gin Mackey
Owls Head, ME

I thanked them profusely as they went on to the next job.

For a few minutes, I stood around admiring the new washer and dryer. I got the Windex and some paper towels and carefully removed a few shreds of glue where a label had been stuck to the top of the washer.

I realized I didn't want to use the washer and dryer. Then they wouldn't be new anymore. All my regular clothes were dirty. I was wearing my good clothes. I knew I'd have to use the washer and dryer sometime. Just not yet.

I found an unusual number of reasons to be in the cellar the rest of the day. I'd go downstairs, get a can of this or that from the storage area. While I was there, I'd look for just a minute at the shiny new appliances.

I held out until that night, then carefully picked out clothes to wash. I pondered the selection of water (cold), cycle (regular) and wash minutes (ten). I hovered while she revved up, filled, rinsed and spun. I moved the squeaky clean wet clothes to the dryer. When I pressed start, she did. I actually thought about pulling a chair up to the dryer and watching it like a television.

I felt like queen for a day. I thought back to the show I had seen so many times as a child. Housewives would win all kinds of things for their homes. They would leap around and cheer and cry and carry on. It would probably be twenty years 'til I needed another washer and dryer. I might as well make the most of it.

I shouted "Whoo-hoo!" and twirled around the basement floor, waving to the invisible, cheering crowd.

Russell Buker
Alexander, ME

Cloudy

while I doggedly
shovel:
could be
any street my icy
feet
have been or will
go.
in positive dreams,
languages
wanting to return
as though
my shadow meets me,
breathless
bird rebuilding itself
shivering
from behind its
veil
of immobile cold,
tired
of living with me,
martyred
on cloudy days
with
aches, pains we all
should
like to be rid of, yes,
without
returning to our
past
or forecasting at
best
a semi-translucent
future

Elmae Passineau
Wausau, WI

Refusing Buttermilk

We called her OlMizButtermilk
  behind her back
  refusing, politely, her offering
  each morning at breakfast
  and suffering her scowls in silence
We had risen at seven
  coolness hurrying our washing and dressing
  and waited, politely, in single file
  to be led down to the dining hall
We prayed, or were prayed over,
  before the meal, after the meal,
  and again at the schoolhouse
We sat up straight, politely attentive,
  wrote our sentences neatly
  read our stories solemnly
  did our numbers diligently
In the playground,
  boys batted or kicked balls
  on the north half
  girls played hopscotch, jumped ropes,
  and rode tire swings on the south
Sometimes in the evening, oh joy!
  MizViolet would read us a story,
  a mystery about stolen diamonds
  and dead bodies washing ashore
  or maybe an adventure
  with a boy and a girl lost in the woods
  and the wolves are closing in,
  but in the end they are always found
  by their mom and dad
  and live happily ever after

(continued)

Elmae Passineau
Wausau, WI

And then we would thank her,
  politely, for the story
  and lie in bed
  dreaming, perhaps,
  that we, too, would be found
  by a mother and a father

***

Lorelee L. Sienkowski
Packwaukee, WI

Lost

A poem, quick written on napkin,
is missing, recalled out of air.
It's hiding on desktop in office
mid flotsam and author despair.

To sort, takes real concentration;
To file, takes even more care,
so, often, things only get riffled—
new stacks take up residence there.

At some point must chaos be tackled,
the first step is sort into class—
"writing" gets poems and essays
and "crafting" gets outcome and task.

Soon chaos has turned into order
and desktop is cleared of the mess,
but writing, unfound, still is missing—
then found as a bookmark, at last.

Jean Biegun
Manitowoc, WI

Book of Job

On days when the sky
is too much,

a small farmhouse
in South Dakota may shiver

and try to hide
under quaking trees.

Tamed fields serene once
will tremble and belch up rocks

when crazed light comes
before prairie storms.

The small farm folds in
on itself,

pressed down by slabs of
unconcerned mustard-colored

clouds.
Life on such a land

underneath a giant sky
is a crossed-fingers

wishbone deal, a bet
Eden maybe will return.

Maureen Anaya
Berwick, ME

Does a Ghost Live Here?

Babs and Harry Hamilton enjoyed renovating old homes. Babs worked as an interior decorator and Harry was employed by a company as a home repair specialist; however, both decided to leave their salaried jobs and work together fixing up old homes to sell for profit.

This lovely autumn day was perfect for viewing old homes for future renovation and they were overjoyed when riding along an old country road they came upon a run-down Victorian mansion with a FOR SALE sign posted outside.

"This would be a real challenge," Harry said.

"Let's go over and have a peek inside," Babs suggested.

"I guess it wouldn't hurt. It looks abandoned."

They approached the house together and just as they were about to look through one partially broken window the creaky front door opened. The small figure of an elderly lady appeared clutching a long shawl around her hunched over body. The pale faced woman with long white hair glanced at the couple and inquired to their presence.

"We saw the FOR SALE sign and were interested in buying the house," Harry explained.

"It's wonderful here. I've lived here a long time. Come inside and have a look," the elderly lady offered.

The couple stepped inside and at first glance were startled at the amount of cobwebs and dust everywhere. Consequently, before viewing the rest of the house they decided to call the real estate company rather than bother the elderly lady unnecessarily.

"We'll check with the real estate office and come back at a later date," Harry stated.

"I'll be here," the elderly lady replied.

As soon as they reached home, Babs texted the real estate office. A reply came through immediately but Babs

Maureen Anaya
Berwick, ME

had a hard time relaying the message to her husband.

"Well, what did they say?" Harry inquired.

"They said the house had been abandoned for years. I wonder who the elderly woman was?"

***

Sherry Ballou Hanson
Portland, OR

The Blue Tree

Deep in my heart
a pilot light burns
in this life, on this walk
through cutting wind
on a frozen January night.
A tiny fir in a wooded copse
loaded with lights smoldering blue
stops me in boot prints
I make through snow
in the labyrinth of my neighborhood,
luminous but all electric,
no mystery or miracle
but a holy stop nonetheless.
We all know angels never rest.

Taylor Leddin
Frankfort, IL

Navy Is My Favorite Color

Often we all fall victim to taking the wonderful gifts we have in life for granted. During the continuity of our daily routines, it is easy to lose focus on what is truly important in life. However, every once in a while, life can hit you and remind you just how lucky you are. For me, I am lucky to have such an amazing family. I am also grateful and take pride in America, this wonderful place we call home where it is an honor to serve your country. I am constantly thankful for the amazing role models I have been able to look up to, especially Jack Leddin.

Jack Leddin is many things. He is a father, a retired employee of the Illinois Bell Phone Company, and a great golfer. He is also my grandfather and he has always been a source of inspiration in my life. One of the most important qualities that Jack holds is that he is a reliable man. You can always count on him to stick to his word and to lend a helping hand. This, among many of his other outstanding qualities, was something that he learned while serving in the United States Navy. In the interim time after he finished school and before he was married, Jack spent four years in the Navy, which he describes as a great time. He joined the Navy by choice after finishing high school as opposed to being drafted by the Army. "Joining any branch of the service I think is one of the greatest things a kid can do if they don't want to go to college because they learn the basic things of discipline, responsibility, and organization. You learn to take care of yourself, be responsible for yourself," says Jack. He also explains that one of the reasons as to why the Navy was so great was because he was able to travel the world, which he may not have been able to do otherwise. During his four years he visited Japan, Korea, and China, and even spent three months living in Hawaii. He worked as an officer on a

Taylor Leddin
Frankfort, IL

destroyer. "Working as an officer was a good job and the ship was very accommodating and very nice," says Jack.

When his four years began coming to a close, Jack had to think about what steps to take next. "I probably would've thought about shipping over at the time. The problem is, when you ship over, you don't really know where you're going to go," he explains with a smile. "They can tell you a lot of wonderful things but you never know for sure." He instead opted to come home and start off a life of his own, meeting, as he kindly puts it, his "sweetheart" and the couple went on to have five kids and ten grandkids. Although Jack decided not to continue life in the Navy, he still looks back fondly at his time in the service and still describes it as one of the best times in his life. His home is filled with mementos from the Navy, ranging from an American flag to a window from the destroyer he had worked on. He made a lot of great friends in the service, as well as some good memories, but most importantly, he learned the skills and qualities of what it takes to make for a great man, which is what he is today. "It had a big impact when you finally got to work and got a job because you have the responsibility to take on a job and you're happy with what you're doing. Especially if you get a job you like," he explains. Jack says that the best part of being in the Navy was the privilege of being able to do it. While his time in the Navy made him proud to be an American, his service and dedication to his country, and his family, has made me proud to be his granddaughter.

Robert B. Moreland
Pleasant Prairie, WI

Amnesia

Fickle February surprise comes when
warm spells erase three months of old snow banks
blackened by road grime, salt and sand. Puddles
erase the bitter hand of winter's grief.
The greening brown patches of grass show through
and for the first time in weeks, there is hope.

Barely two weeks ago, frigid gales howled
against this small cottage, rattling glass panes.
The wind chill, twenty below, flurries flew;
darkened clouds obscuring the crescent moon.
The witch of winter stole away good will.

Yet when it was almost too much to bear,
balmy days came, first time above freezing.
Mourning doves coo on the feeder, grateful;
a pair of blue jays extol life's goodness.

Bright sunshine banishes gloomy moods,
crocuses lift their heads. The mile long ice floe
melts into the bluest great lake, sand reappears.
For the briefest moment, heartbreaks vanish,
love is new and anything is possible.

Sylvia Little-Sweat
Wingate, NC

Pockets

At first light the gray
December day I wore
Mother's coat outside,
its pockets—like each
morning's waking
thought—caught me
by surprise. In a
selvage of fleece lay
a wooden toothpick
Mother had salvaged.
The other pocket held
a Kleenex wadded like
a ball. That was all—
mundane things that
suddenly became
rare reliquaries of my
mother's daily needs.
Seeking warmth, my
fingers felt, instead,
the wordless
Braille of grief.

***

Stasis

Gray-robed with a cowl
of snow, Saint Francis holds cold
Winter in his arms.

Helen Ackermann
Rothschild, WI

Firmly Rooted

The journal entry for May 10, 1949 revealed the following, "Planting evergreen trees today. Got 75 of them from a neighbor. Three rows, we planted and they sure look pretty. It's like a dream. I always wanted evergreen trees so I got them now." The journal excerpt comes from my father's journal. The entries were not long and often were a report on the weather as well as on the many tasks that were a part of running a small dairy farm in northern Wisconsin.

I have always loved trees. That love of trees began as a small child probably because I helped my father plant those trees. I was only four years old. I remember the care he took with each planting, digging a hole and carefully inserting the seedling making sure the roots were well covered. I think it was my job to pour in some water.

If I were asked to describe some of the specific trees that have held a place in my heart, it would be relatively easy to do. The first would be a cottonwood from the old farmstead. My grandfather planted a willow grove when he first came to northwestern Wisconsin from the flat lands of North Dakota. At each end of the willow grove he planted some cottonwoods. They stood as sentinels marking the grove. Eventually, the farm was sold, the buildings razed and now all that remains is one cottonwood.

Another tree that holds a special place in my heart is the pine that still stands in what was an empty lot across the street from where we raised our sons. Again, nothing is left of the house or other houses on the dead-end street as all properties were sold to an industrial firm. For some reason the pine was left standing. I could see our sons and their friends playing baseball near the pine from our dining room window. Although it stands stately and tall still, there are no longer children there to enjoy its beauty.

Helen Ackermann
Rothschild, WI

The tree across from the school building where our sons received their elementary education is the third tree I hold dear. It is a tall spruce but was only ten feet tall when I became the principal of the school. It is a handsome tree that provided a hiding place for many children whom I came to know and love. Although long retired, when I drive by, I still see children sitting under its branches protected from wind and sun.

Finally, the fourth tree that is special to me is the large white pine in our backyard. We have many trees on our property, but this one is a giant. It towers over the house and during a storm, there is always the thought if the wind is strong, might it not come down upon the house? In twenty years, however, that has not happened. It is surrounded by other trees giving it some protection and we continue to take our chances. I can see it from my office and often watch the birds and squirrels that love it too.

Trees can give us a sense of rootedness. As they sink their roots into the ground they secure themselves firmly. Don't we do the same? We sink our roots into a ground of divine being, a mystery called creation. We grow, we age, we develop into a being that might be buffeted by the storms of life but we continue on, rooted deeply in the divine mystery we call life. We experience the joy of the rising sun, the gentle rains and the depth of cold here in northern Wisconsin that threatens to freeze our very strength. Hopefully, as we pass through this existence, there are many times when we give shelter to others, inviting them to find solace and comfort under our branches.

Bonnie Feuer
Orange, CT

Looking Skyward—Remembering Mom

Always interested in astronomy, and sky gazing all my life, I was frustrated that I had never witnessed a shooting star. Friends would return from trips out west with tales of the most gorgeous skies, lit with the stars' activities. Even here, in the east, I would often hear casual reports of people enjoying the breathtaking, darting lights.

On a crisp and icy midnight in December, the phone call came that told me my mother was very close to death. Emerging into the brisk and empty night, I looked to the sky for comfort. The stars were brilliant, but still, and I chose to wish upon the glimmering one that seemed closest to my home. With the childish hope of those who believe in such wishes, I asked for an end to my mother's many years of suffering with Alzheimer's disease.

At the nursing home, I found her in bed, lying on her right side, in fetal position. Overcome by a resigned sense of calmness, I held her hand and gave her permission to leave me. I reviewed many of the best times of her life, and thanked her for all that had been warm and constant in mine. Softly, in the background, from the speakers in the hallway, my mind registered a familiar song.

Six hours later, in the gentle way she had lived her life, my mother departed. I became busy in the hyper way of those absorbing pain, running from one errand to another, while refusing to let anyone do anything for me. Alone, in the car, the song from the previous night suddenly came forward in my mind with clarity. Chills flowed from my spine to the skin on my arms, making me shudder, as I recalled the scene in my mother's room. While I had said my last "Good-bye" to my mother, these words had been playing outside her door. "If the world should stop revolving, spinning slowing down to die; I'd spend the end with you, and when the world was

Bonnie Feuer
Orange, CT

through...One by one the stars would all go out, then you and I, would simply fly away."

Three months after my mother's death, in a melancholy mood, I went outside, late at night. Wrapped in a blanket, I sat alone under a deep, royal sky. Looking to the stars, I decided that the one outshining the rest represented my mother. Sighing and feeling sorry for myself, I sat there for nearly an hour, staring at my personal star. Then, with silence as my only witness, I watched it soar through the sky, and gracefully disappear. My eyes filled as I whispered, "Thank you, Mom."

Time, with its medicinal way has brought me to a more peaceful place. I recently looked upward on a clear, chilly night and realized that lately, I notice more than the stars. A thin and luminous crescent sliced the sky with a smile.

***

Maude Olsen
South Bristol , ME

Hindsight

As I looked out one morning,
 Before the sun was high,
 There was a streak of silver
 Floating in the sky.

 It looked like errant moonshine
 And then it came to mind:
 That silly old moon had gone to bed
 And left himself behind!

Julia W. Ridge
Portland, ME

The Live-Day Long

The mother-linnet in the brake
Bewails her ravish'd young;
So I, for my lost darling's sake,
Lament the live-day long.
—From "A Mother's Lament on the Death of Her Son,"
by Robert Burns

On a cold late December afternoon in Maine, my brother Brian tried to kill himself, again. It was mid 1990's. Brian was 50, unemployed and renting a room at our ma's house. Police found him face down, reeking of alcohol as blood seeped from his gut onto the wooden ties of the railroad tracks a mile from Ma's. Brian had impaled himself on the end of a serrated kitchen knife. They rushed him to the hospital in a nearby town, where he was stitched up and transferred to the psych ward.

The Ashes

Ma brought Brian's ashes from Maine to Boston. In the car, she looked out the window; her mouth stiff, the corners turned down.

In the mid-sixties, after Brian got out of the Navy, he had settled in Boston on Joy Street. He was there until he moved to Maine in 1975.

Now, Ma and I rode along Storrow Drive. It was the beginning of March, still winter, so the rain was cold and thick, pummeling the car. At times, when we were stopped in traffic, the downpour stifled our voices when we tried to talk. I scanned the side of the road looking for a place to pull over. It would be somewhere near the Arthur Fiedler Bridge, I knew that much.

"There," she said. I followed Ma's look, as we approached

Julia W. Ridge
Portland, ME

the Fiedler Bridge, to a spit of land with anchoring scrub and jutting out in to the Charles River. Just beyond the land was a mooring with sailboats.

The biting east wind had turned the rain to sleet and snow. As Ma opened her door at the curb where we were to get out, a gust wrestled the door from her hand and blew it wide open. This made her wince. She turned up the collar of her blue quilted coat and wrapped a scarf around it. When she stepped out of the car, a deep pool of slush covered much of her leather boot with its faux fur trim and left a wet stain. She looked down, then looked up at me and shrugged. "No matter," she said.

Ma kept Brian's ashes in a small wooden box inside her purse, which she held against her abdomen, as if to keep the box from the wind, as if to absorb its contents, carry them to term, and start all over again. From her purse she pulled a picture of Brian standing by trees with sailboats behind him with a note on the back that was hard to decipher. It read, "At a Pop's concert." Ma used it like a map and pointed past me toward the river.

The first time Brian attempted he was 20 and serving time in the Navy. It was the early sixties, before the escalation of Vietnam. He was a peacetime recruit. Brian tried to jump off the balcony in the lobby of a Chicago hotel. Someone stopped him. A Navy official called Ma to let her know. She kept this to herself for years.

There wasn't much time before dark. Ma and I hurried along the sidewalk and under the bridge to the paved pathway that led to a small bridge over a retaining pond. We stopped to get our bearings.

After a few days of psychological evaluation in the hospital, Brian entered a mandatory counseling program. Brian was encouraged to write his feelings down, to get his thoughts on paper and out of his head. The writing, the counselors told us, would be instrumental to Brian's recovery.

I went to visit Brian in the psych ward a few days before

Julia W. Ridge
Portland, ME

he was discharged and ready to start outpatient counseling. He sat at a desk against the wall. He turned to look at me when I walked in. He had a pencil in his right hand, which was resting on a writing pad. Except for the pad and Brian's hands, the desk was bare. A wastebasket next to the desk overflowed with crumpled pieces of lined paper.

Brian got up to go to the bathroom, and I leaned over the desk to read the small, barely legible words on the paper: "My name is Brian," was all he had written. He had been in the hospital eight days.

In the waning light by the river's edge, Ma's taut face turned gray. She stopped and handed me the photo. In the picture, Brian stood near a cluster of trees with sailboats in the background.

"Over there," she said again.

We walked out to the middle of the small point of land. Ma eased the box from her bag and cupped it in her gloved hands. Her eyes filled. Then Ma opened the box and shook the small fragments of bone and ashes around the scrub. Ma whispered, "Goodbye, Brian. Be happy"—her voice filled with the same trepidation as any mother when she bids goodbye to her son on his first day of school; as any mother when she surrenders her child to the universe.

In the outpatient program the counselors reported to us on Brian's progress. They told us he had joined a group in which he had begun to open up and talk about himself. They were small steps, 'but steps,' they said.

Without insurance, the outpatient treatments were tempo-rary. As a veteran, though, Brian was entitled to treatment at a veterans hospital. We made arrangements for Brian to be admitted to an in-residence program in Maine.

After two weeks there, Brian called me at home. It was late afternoon early February. Before I finished saying hello he said, 'Ya know, if you haven't served on the front lines, they treat you like shit. They won't give me meds. Get me outta here.' I told him I would make arrangements to be up there in

Julia W. Ridge
Portland, ME

another day or two. And, although Brian's victim-perspective was nothing new, the flat tone in his voice alarmed me.

That night, at midnight, Brian skulked through the corridors of the hospital. After he reached the stairwell and jogged down the steps to the first floor—passed the orderlies and the skeleton crew on the third shift—after he told the person at the front desk he was 'gettin' out of this hell-hole,' Brian muscled through the doors he had entered ten days earlier and walked out into the dark. He trudged through the deep snow that covered the long driveway of the remote facility to a road, where he headed west and hiked six miles to the nearest town.

No one asked him where he was going. No one followed him to the door. No one, this time, tried to save him.

On that subzero February night, Brian found a fire escape attached to a building in the middle of the town. He climbed to the top. He held his duffel bag, filled with his belongings, and jumped from the iron platform to the ice and snow below.

His body lay twisted and broken, his head cocked to one side. The duffel bag he carried was next to him, the stitching at the zipper ripped open, the contents strewn across the snow: Cassettes of Frank Sinatra, Ricky Nelson and Elvis in plastic casings, cracked and shattered; Two books, Norman Mailer's 'Marilyn Monroe' and Mario Puzo's 'The Godfather,' splayed out on either side of him, spines broken and pages face down, soaked to fragility. His sneakers and a note were all that remained in his bag.

In the police report, the policeman who found him wrote, 'Could not read note. Just scribble.'

It had turned dark by the time Ma and I began our walk to the center of the city. The whirling wind walloped us as we climbed Beacon Hill. I pulled Ma snug to me and we pushed against the stubborn gale to Faneuil Hall, the sleet pelting our faces like tiny slaps.

"Are you cold?" I asked.

"No," she said. And Ma lifted her face, giving it to the sleet as it hit her, taking it as if it was hers to take.

GOOSE RIVER ANTHOLOGY, 2016

We seek selections of fine poetry, essays, and short stories (3,000 words or less) for the 14th annual *Goose River Anthology, 2016.* The book will be beautifully produced with full color cover and full color dust jacket for hard covers.

You may submit even if you have been published before in a previous edition of the *Goose River Anthology.* We retain one-time publishing rights. All rights revert back to the author after publication. You may submit as many pieces as you like.

EARN CASH ROYALTIES. Author will receive a 10% royalty on all sales that he or she generates.

There is no purchase required and nothing is required of the author for publication. Deadline for submissions is April 30, 2016. Publication will be in the fall of 2016 (they make great Christmas gifts). Guidelines are as follows:

- Submit clean, typed copy by snail mail—**mandatory**
- Email a Word or rtf file to us (if possible)
- Reading fee: $1.00 per page
- Do not put two poems on the same page
- Essays and short stories should be double-spaced
- **SASE for notification** (one forever stamp) plus additional postage for possible return of submission if desired.
- Author's name & address at top of each page of paper copy and first page of emailed copies.

Submit to:
Goose River Anthology, 2016
3400 Friendship Road
Waldoboro, ME 04572-6337
E mail: gooseriverpress@roadrunner.com
www.gooseriverpress.com

CPSIA information can be obtained at www.ICGtesting.com
Printed in the USA
BVOW02s0430150915

417733BV00002B/2/P